Love from
Alice
xx

A.A. WOODWARD
PUBLISHING

SECOND TIME HAPPY -1

SECOND TIME HAPPY

A.A.Woodward

SECOND TIME HAPPY -3

For Nancy & Fred, with love,

and for all who served, with gratitude.

AUTHOR'S NOTE

This story is written in loving and ever-grateful memory of all who served and supported the war effort between 1939 and 1945. It is inspired by real people and real events of that extraordinary time, though told here through a blend of history and fiction.

The real people behind this tale are Nancy and Fred Oakes. Fred served aboard *HMS Ramillies*, while Nancy was a Wren (WRNS – Women's Royal Naval Service) stationed in Scotland. Their lives, like those of so many, were shaped by the trials and sacrifices of war. Secondary characters are fictitious.

For the purposes of this narrative, I have chosen *HMS Fury* to align with the timeline of the story, weaving together fact and imagination to bring their world to life. *HMS Fury* (H76) had a busy and dangerous 1944 before her final service off the coast of Normandy. Other events and elements of this book are based on true life events, from stories shared first hand from Nancy Oakes (Great Grandmother).

The title 'Second Time Happy' comes from the U-boat hunting patrols of the North Atlantic, which the Axis powers called '*first time happy*' during an initial period of successful patrols and '*second time happy*' when war was also declared on America, suggesting a following successful period of patrols. For this story, it also carries a more personal meaning: the courage to love again after loss, as Nancy does in this story.

This book is not intended as a strict historical record, but as a tribute to the courage, endurance, and quiet heroism of a generation.

THE SILENCE AND THE STATIC

February 1944 – Scotland.

The signal room never slept. the blackout curtains trapped the stale, cold air, and the glow of shaded lamps cast sharp shadows across rows of bent figures. The smell was always the same: damp wool, cigarette smoke, hot dust from the wireless valves. Nancy sat hunched at her desk, headphones clamped tight to her ears, pencil poised above her pad.

Nancy's wrist ached from the constant note-taking, but she pressed on, her handwriting sharp and precise. She had long since trained herself not to think of the voices behind the signals, whether friendly or enemy. Each coded word was a piece of a larger puzzle, and her duty was to capture it without falter. Still, sometimes, as she lifted her pencil from the page, she felt the weight of what those words meant—convoys rerouted, ships in peril, lives hanging in the balance. She swallowed hard and forced her mind back to discipline. Emotion had no place here, she told herself, though it was never entirely absent.

Crackling static filled the lines. She strained to separate it, heart ticking faster as the bursts of German code began to emerge — clipped, urgent, full of menace.

"Got one," she muttered, she leaned forwards, scribbling fast, marking the sequence onto her pad. Her fingers ached from the chill, but she wrote smoothly, steady, fearful of missing a syllable. Somewhere out there, beyond the dark sea, ships depended on her hands keeping steady. Three sequences of numbers, then silence. The hair prickled on the back of her neck. U-boat chatter. She recognised the pattern now, after long months at her post. Somewhere out in the dark sea, men in steel coffins were hunting.

Nancy passed the slip to the petty officer on duty. Jack White, he barely glanced up, already reaching for the red telephone. Routine. For him, perhaps. For her, it was never routine. Every number, every call sign, was a shadow of ships at sea — convoys carrying food, fuel, men. Dependent on her, dependent on all of the Wrens on duty, to hear every flicker, record every mark, to never miss, and always be accurate. Sometimes she wandered, between the silence and the static, if one of those escorts she was listening out to protect was *his*.

She bit her lip, refocusing on the static. She must not think of him here. Duty came first.

However, Fred Harding's face surfaced in her mind anyway — the way he had looked at her at the dance weeks ago, as if he saw something solid in her when she felt nothing but hollow. She had not meant to let him in. Not after Edward.

A knot grew and twisted in Nancy's stomach, taking all her concentration. Edward's laugh still haunted the corners of her mind. Edward in uniform,

Edward striding off with that unshakable confidence, Edward whose name had been etched into stone far too soon. She had sworn she would never do this again — never give her heart to someone the sea or the war could so easily take. A first love is difficult to lose, and difficult to replace, guilt tugged at the knot inside her.

Edward had gone down with HMS *Hood*, swallowed in a single terrible moment when the Bismarck's shells tore her open in the cold Atlantic. Out of more than a thousand men, only three were pulled alive from the wreckage. Edward wasn't one of them. His body was never recovered; the sea kept him, leaving Nancy with nothing but a name on a memorial and the echo of a laugh that would never come again.

Nancy's mind swam with thoughts and feelings. Conflict. To ground herself, organise her thoughts, Nancy reached into her breast pocket of her heavy uniform jacket, and in a second of steady peace she rubbed her thumb across a small folded piece of paper she stored safely.

Fred had written. A short note, folded neatly: *You make the dark nights seem lighter*. She carried it in her pocket now, a dangerous little flame against her chest. On occasion, Nancy would find herself reaching into her pocket, just to touch her thumb against the little piece of paper, to ensure it is still in position, safe where she left it. Habitual. Becoming more and more like a comfort blanket each day that passed. Nancy's mind wandered, it took her back to Fred, his tall figure, his kind, smiling face, the dimples in his cheeks from his smile, his bright, blue eyes and his curly, messy light brown hair.

The wireless static crackled against her ear, the noise was the kind that would send anyone to sleep, before another interruption. Nancy held firm, scratching quickly the code flooding her ears. Before again passing the note to Jack. "Strong signal, 23:57 hours, 12 MHz band, presumed Kriegsmarine." He announced aloud to the telephone after conveying the letters and sequence from Nancy's note.

Another Wren, Mary, exhaled a shaky breath beside her, lifting her eyes to Nancy, and giving a subtle nod. Nancy realised she'd been holding her own.

Mary was barely twenty, with a round face that could never quite hide her emotions. Her dark hair always escaped from under her cap, curling in wisps no matter how sharply she pinned it. She laughed easily, sometimes too loudly in the mess, and had a knack for lifting the mood even on the darkest of days.

She was quick with the wireless, her fingers nimble, her handwriting neat, though she sometimes doubted herself when the pressure mounted. Nancy saw it at once — the nervous way Mary bit her lip when she thought she'd made an error, the relief in her eyes when someone reassured her. From the first week, Nancy had taken her under her wing, steadying her, guiding her, reminding her that sharpness and courage could be quiet brilliant things too.

Nancy had quickly taken a shine to Mary. There was something about her fresh-faced eagerness, the way she spoke with such bright conviction about doing her part after her brother had been drafted into the army. Mary was young, but not naïve—her excitement to help was grounded in a courage that Nancy admired. In the mess and uncertainty of war, Mary's presence felt like a spark of warmth, a reminder of what they were all working for. She was earnest, determined, and quick to laugh, and Nancy found herself drawing strength from that quiet resilience.

Mary adored stories — devoured library books, passed dog-eared magazines across the bunks, whispered tales of film stars and romances to keep spirits up on long shifts. She had a habit of teasing Nancy, gently pushing her about Fred whenever the subject came near. Yet beneath the chatter and brightness, there was a softer thread: a girl far from home, masking her fear with laughter.

To Nancy, Mary was both a sister and a shadow of herself years before — full of hope, untested by loss, still believing the war couldn't touch her too deeply. That, more than anything, was why Nancy felt she had to protect her.

The clock ticked loudly on the wall. Midnight. Another convoy was running the gauntlet of U-boats tonight. For all she knew, Fred's destroyer could be among them.

The next morning Nancy woke in her bunk, a dark room, with no natural light, giving the feeling of being underground, and offering no indication of time. The room was cold, the coal stove barely touching the chill, but filling the air with the smell of burning coals, masking the damp aroma from the woollen blankets.

Nancy rolled her head to her small clock beside her bed, on registering the time she quietly tapped the underside of the bunk above her. Shuffling and a deep sigh. "There is no way it is time to wake up yet" Mary whispered quietly in response to Nancy's tap. Nancy lay quietly, a small smile on her face, she couldn't help but share the feeling.

"Let us go and have some breakfast" Nancy started in a quiet whisper, conscious other girls were still sleeping. "I am ready to eat after last nights shift". A groan of reluctant agreement came from the bunk above, before Mary climbed down.

"Porridge again" Mary remarked as they walked side by side into the mess. Nancy couldn't help but smile, roll her eyes and shake her head at the sarcasm.

"At this point, I would eat anything, I felt even more on-edge last night than usual. I think food will make me feel a little better. Maybe it'll put some life back into you too"!

Tray in hand, Mary looked to Nancy, her eyes puffy and glazed "I think maybe some fresh air would do me some good. Perhaps we go for a wander before our day shift"? Nancy nodded her head in agreement.

Sat on the benches in the mess, Nancy and Mary devoured their warm porridge, without time for pleasant exchange.

The mess hall was a cavernous space, its high ceiling lined with exposed beams and strung with low-hanging bulbs that cast a yellowish, uneven glow across the room. Long rows of wooden benches and trestle tables filled the centre, scarred by years of use, initials carved into the surfaces by restless hands. At one end, the serving counter stretched beneath a row of frosted windows, panes rattling faintly whenever the wind caught them.

The place was never quiet. The scrape of cutlery against tin plates echoed from every corner, a constant undercurrent to the clatter of pans from behind the counter. Voices rose and fell in waves—laughter, chatter, the occasional burst of song—threads of conversation that tangled together until they became a single, rolling hum. Every so often, the clang of a dropped ladle or the sharp call of an officer cut through the din, snapping attention back to order before the swell of noise returned.

Despite the hard benches and plain walls, the mess hall offered a sense of community. Men and women crammed shoulder to shoulder, nudging for space, sharing gossip from the latest letters, or retelling the same old jokes with just enough exaggeration to make them new again. The atmosphere busy, a little chaotic, yet oddly comforting—an anchor of familiarity amidst the uncertainty of their days. Wrens and sailors alike felt the pulse of the base, where weariness and camaraderie met over chipped mugs and dented plates, lit by the flicker of bulbs swaying on their cords.

The mess hall still smelled faintly of porridge and weak tea when Nancy and Mary slipped out into the morning air. The sky was pale, streaked with thin clouds, the kind of washed-out light that made the whole base look colourless.

Mary linked her arm through Nancy's as they strolled toward the edge of the harbour. Nancy had traded her navy-blue uniform for the plain civvies she kept carefully folded at the bottom of her trunk. That morning she wore a calf-length wool skirt in heather grey, sensible enough for the damp grass but still neat against her figure. Her blouse was cream, the collar softened by wear, and over it she pulled a dark cardigan, mended at the cuff where the wool had frayed. She'd knotted a patterned scarf around her neck — faded rose and blue, one of the few colourful things she owned — and tucked her hands into leather gloves that had grown supple with use. "If I stay in that hut another hour, I'll start hearing Morse in my sleep," she sighed. "Dot-dot-dash in my dreams, can you imagine?"

Nancy managed a smile against the bitter wind. "I already do."

Mary, clearly trying to lighten Nancy's mood, lowering her voice, and darting her eyes theatrically to the sea, "You know, I keep thinking if a U-boat captain ever peeked through his periscope here, he'd see us Wrens and abandon the war entirely. 'No, boys, turn around—we can't fight a navy defended by girls with stockings and too much lipstick.'"

"Too much lipstick? Speak for yourself." Nancy replied with a grin on her face.

"Well, you wear yours properly. I end up looking like I've wrestled an octopus." Mary laughed.

The path crunched under their boots, gulls wheeling overhead, their cries sharp against the low drone of generators from the base. Across the water, grey shapes of warships rocked gently at anchor. The sight was both comforting and ominous: guardians, but also reminders of what lay beyond the horizon.

Mary pulled her scarf tighter. "Sometimes I forget there's a world outside all this. Do you ever think about it, Nance? What we'll do when it's over?"

Nancy hesitated. She thought of Edward, of the future they'd once planned — a cottage, a garden, a dog. She thought of Fred, his steady gaze across the dance floor, the words she'd never dared to speak. The ache in her chest made it hard to breathe.

"I think about it," she said at last, her voice soft. "But it feels like tempting fate."

Mary gave her a sideways look, her usual brightness tempered by something gentler. "Maybe, but I think we need to dream a little, or else we'll go mad." She nudged Nancy with her shoulder. "So, when the war's over, what's the first thing you'll do?"

Nancy let out a slow breath, watching it mist in the chill air. "Walk without listening for sirens." Nancy tucked her hair behind her ears in an attempt to tidy it out of her face. The wind however, had other ideas.

Mary laughed, the sound ringing out over the harbour. "Simple, but fair."

They walked on in silence for a while, the gulls wheeling, the ships swaying. For a fleeting moment, Nancy let herself imagine it: a world without static in her ears, without losses marked in pencil. A world where she might walk like this every morning, perhaps accompanied by a dog – Nancy always wanted a dog – most importantly, feeling unafraid.

The sound of a distant gun carried on the wind, pulled her back from her pleasant day-dream. The war was never far.

Nancy looked out to sea, the dark grey waves swelling, topped with icy white frosting. The cold rushed through her body. Somewhere, they're both out there. With that thought, reality hit again. With Mary's arm still linked around hers, she wheeled around and headed back towards base.

The evening shift loomed closer, as Nancy walked through the narrow hallway – a rabbit warren of dim lit tunnels and doorways – towards the signals room, already Nancy could hear the static, the crackle and the sharp blips between the silence.

Sat over her station, eyes down, her head resting on her left hand. The wireless shrieked suddenly, jerking her back to the present. Another signal burst through, louder this time, urgent. She caught fragments — bearing, numbers, a convoy call sign. Her heart skipped. Was it *his*?

Nancy's pencil flew, but before she could pass the slip across, a dull tremor shuddered through the floor. The overhead lamp flickered. Then, faint but distinct, came the far-off thud of guns.

The room froze. Someone whispered, "Raid?"

The petty officer on duty snapped, "Back to your posts. Eyes sharp."

Nancy forced her hand steady again, but her pulse hammered. Outside, the night was no longer quiet. The war was coming closer.

THE PRESENCE OF FURY

The Atlantic was black glass beneath the destroyer's bow the night so clear it made the stars feel close enough to touch. The swell rolling endlessly from horizon to horizon. The great, intimidating destroyer cut through it like a blade, her grey walled bow heaving, spray hissing across the deck. Her presence known and intimidating. Fred stood on the bridge, collar turned up against the cold wind, eyes fixed on the faint smudge of merchant ships ploughing ahead.

Thirty of them. His responsibility was to keep them alive. Tankers, freighters, liberty ships, heavy with food, fuel, and men — a lifeline stretching toward Britain. A feast for the wolves beneath.

Inside the ship, the air was hot and close, smelling of oil, damp clothes, and men who had been too long without fresh water. The mess deck was a jumble of mugs, hammocks slung tight, boots hanging from hooks. Laughter rose in bursts, too loud, too brittle, the kind of laughter men used when silence would let the fear in.

"If this ship rolls one more time, I'll be feeding the fishes again." Fred heard Seaman Barker exclaim, his face pale as chalk.

Fred knew the fear was there. He saw it in the eyes of the younger ratings, lads barely out of school, clutching tea mugs as if warmth alone could keep the sea at bay. Some tried bravado, swapping dirty jokes, puffing cigarettes with studied ease. Others sat quietly, staring at nothing, listening for the sound everyone dreaded: the thump of a torpedo.

Fred caught out of the corner of his eye, stoker Jameson, holding a badly shrunk jumper: "Washed it once, and look at this—fit for a ruddy child now." He announced to a nearby group.

Signalman Peters took the opportunity to respond "Good! You'll look dashing when you join the Sea Scouts." Sending up a roar of laughter.

The destroyer was fast, agile, her engines thundering with each surge, but Fred knew how fragile she really was. One good hit, and she'd go down in minutes. He'd seen it before — ships swallowed whole, men screaming in the freezing dark, their cork vests useless against the cold.

A low murmur of voices drifted around him — lookouts calling bearings, the petty officer checking course. The rhythm was confident, practiced, but Fred's jaw ached from the tension he refused to show. Somewhere out there, invisible in the dark, were U-boats. He could almost feel them, like wolves pacing the edges of the convoy, waiting for a moment to strike.

"Contact!" The cry snapped through the intercom, the sonar operator's voice tight. "Bearing green thirty. Faint, but moving. Range closing."

Fred's jaw clenched. The bridge crew stiffened, every man listening, waiting. Every nerve in Fred's body snapped to attention. His heart beat faster, but his voice came out steady. He gave the order quietly, evenly, as if calm alone could keep the sea from erupting into fire. "Bring her about. Sound action stations."

The klaxon wailed. Boots pounded on steel. Depth charges were primed, the deck alive with shouts. The destroyer swung hard, slicing into the swell, hunting the shadow below.

Fred gripped the rail, the cold biting into his hands, his eyes scanning the black sea. He felt it more than saw it — the presence of men beneath the waves, listening, waiting, patient as death. Somewhere down there, a German commander was lining them up, finger poised on the firing key.

The men trusted him to keep calm, to give them orders, to guide them through the night. Fred thought briefly of Nancy. Of her quiet eyes across the dance hall, the weight she carried in silence. He forced the image aside. Now was not the time for sentiment.

Orders rang out. "Stand by… drop!"

The ship shuddered as the charges tumbled over the stern, hissing into the sea. Seconds stretched into eternity. Then the water erupted in white fountains, the thunder rolling across the convoy. Men held their breath.

Nothing. No wreckage, no oil, no scream of tearing metal. The U-boat had slipped away.

Fred let out a slow breath, the knot in his chest loosening just enough. Around him, the men began to move again, muttering, their nerves frayed but intact. He straightened, voice firm.

"Back on station. Keep sharp. They're out there."

As the destroyer swung back into her screen, Fred fixed his gaze on the convoy. The merchantmen steamed on, black shapes against black water, oblivious to the teeth snapping at their heels.

This hunt had only begun.

The calm didn't last.

Fred was still on the bridge when the call came, a sharp voice through the intercom from the stern lookout:

"Light! Starboard quarter — torpedo wake!"

"Hard a 'port!" Fred barked before the officer of the watch could even repeat it. The destroyer heeled violently, her bow swinging into the swell. The wake of the torpedo sliced white across the dark water, rushing past their stern so close Fred swore he could feel the sea shiver.

No time to breathe. A second streak cut across the convoy's flank. This one hit.

The dull thud shook the air, followed by the monstrous crack of steel splitting. A freighter ahead lurched, fire blooming from her hull. The convoy scattered, the neat line of ships breaking apart in panic.

"Action stations!" The klaxon shrieked. Men poured onto the deck, racing to their guns. Depth charges were primed, steel bars clanking as the crews maneuvered the huge cylinders into place.

Fred grabbed the voice pipe. "Sonar — give me her bearing!"

"Contact bearing red twenty-five, range closing!"

"Engage!"

The destroyer roared forward, the sea spraying cold across the bridge. The first string of depth charges thundered over the stern, the sea erupting behind them in columns of white spray. The men held their breath, waiting for the telltale plume of oil, the twisted wreckage that meant a kill.

Nothing.

Fred's jaw tightened. Fists clenched. His whole-body tense. The U-boat had slipped under them. Somewhere in that black abyss, a German commander was listening, waiting for the perfect angle to strike again.

Another explosion shook the convoy — this time to port. A tanker burst into flame, a towering fireball turning the night into day. The smell of burning fuel hit Fred's nostrils, acrid and choking.

Sailors cried out, pointing. Men were in the water, tiny figures thrashing in the firelit sea, their cork vests glowing orange against the inferno. Fred forced himself to look away. The faint screams of men could be heard between the clashes of metal and booming, panicked footsteps onboard. He couldn't stop for them. Not yet.

"Bring her about — shallow sweep!"

The destroyer swung again, her engines screaming. More charges crashed into the deep, the deck rattling under the recoil of her guns as they fired at shadows. The crew moved with frantic precision — young men, teeth clenched, eyes wide, each action drilled into their bones.

Fred steadied his hands on the handrail. He had to be the calm in the storm, even as fear gnawed at him. If his voice cracked, if his orders faltered, the men would know. Then they would break.

The sea boiled behind them, columns of spray reaching for the sky. For a heartbeat, silence reigned. Then came the muffled roar of something rupturing below, and a smear of oil rose to the surface. The iridescent slick lit up by the fires of boats burning around them.

The men erupted, cheers breaking through the night. A kill. Maybe.

Fred didn't cheer. He watched the flames devouring the freighter, the shapes still struggling in the water, and felt the weight settle heavy in his gut. In the pit of his stomach, one thought burned hotter than the rest: If they went down here, Nancy would never even know where to mourn him.

They had survived the first strike, yes — but the wolves were still out there, and the night was far from over.

Dawn crept reluctantly across the Atlantic, a pale grey light spilling over the waves. The convoy limped onward, smaller now, gaps in the line where ships had been the night before. The smoke still lingered on the horizon, a black smear against the sky.

Fred stood on the bridge, his oilskin stiff with salt. He hadn't slept, hadn't even sat down. The men around him looked just as hollow-eyed, their movements sluggish with exhaustion. The adrenaline of battle had drained away, leaving only the weight.

"Two freighters gone, one tanker burning astern," the officer of the watch reported quietly. "God knows how many men in the water."

Fred nodded once. He didn't ask for the numbers. He didn't need them. He could still hear the cries echoing across the dark — men shouting for help, cut off mid-breath as the sea claimed them. He had forced himself to turn away, abruptly. If he looked too long, he'd lose more than just the convoy.

The flames, reflected in Fred's eyes.

On deck below, the survivors gathered, hunched in their greatcoats, clutching enamel mugs of tea that steamed in the cold air. Some joked weakly, their laughter brittle. Others sat in silence, staring into space, God only knows the feelings they were feeling, the thoughts they were thinking, the scenes they were replaying in their minds.

Fred forced himself to move among the men, speaking evenly, offering a word here, a hand on a shoulder there. They needed to see their officer steady, unshaken. That was his duty: to carry the fear for them.

When he climbed back to the bridge and the wind cut across his face, his mask slipped for just a moment. He gripped the rail until his knuckles whitened, staring at the void where the lost ships should have been.

He whispered under his breath, a vow the sea alone could hear:

Not again. Not if I can stop it.

Deep inside, he knew the truth — the wolves would come again. Next time, it might be his ship dragged under.

As dawn broke, Fred watched the convoy limp on, ships missing from the line. By evening, the reports would be carried to a signals hut in Scotland, and Nancy would see the losses written cold in ink.

⚓

The signals hut was icy, the paraffin stove long since sputtered out. Nancy deflated, sat at her desk, rubbing at the ache in her wrist as the duty officer read from the morning reports. His voice was flat, brisk — a list of losses, nothing more.

"Two freighters sunk. One tanker ablaze, presumed lost. Survivors taken off where possible. Convoy continues."

The words scratched across the paper as Nancy copied them, her pencil biting hard enough to tear the page. She kept her face still, but her stomach twisted. The convoy. Fred's convoy?

Mary leaned over, solemn faced, whispering just loud enough for Nancy to hear. "It's awful, isn't it? All those poor souls."

Nancy nodded, her throat too tight to reply. She wanted to ask the question that burned in her chest — the escorts? Were the destroyers hit? Was

Fred's ship among them? But she couldn't. They weren't supposed to ask, not here. They were supposed to be impartial, professional. The war didn't allow for personal fears.

Still, as she filed the report, her eyes caught on the jagged gap in the convoy's numbers. Ships that had been there yesterday, gone now. Just as Edward had been — there one moment, gone the next, leaving nothing but silence and a carved name.

Nancy forced herself back to the wireless, adjusting the dial, pencil poised. Static hissed in her ears. Every signal, every code she wrote down could be the thread that kept another ship alive. She clung to that thought like a lifeline.

Deep inside, she whispered the prayer she could never voice aloud:

Please, not Fred. Don't take him too.

LIFE AND SURVIVAL

For Fred, life on the destroyer became a pattern he could almost measure time by. Each day began with the same call, the same shuffle of hammocks being stowed, the same smell of oil and salt on the air. He would rise with the others, boots thudding softly on steel decking, the ship alive beneath his feet with the constant thrum of her engines. That constant, rhythmic, vibration was both a comfort and a reminder—so long as he felt it, they were moving, surviving.

His watches blurred together in long stretches of sea and sky. At the wheel, his hands moved almost without thought, steering her through swell and spray, his eyes fixed forward. When he stood lookout, binoculars pressed to his brow, every shadow on the horizon seemed to hold a question. Most days, the sea was only the sea, and yet Fred never let himself forget that danger could appear in an instant.

The mess offered its own kind of rhythm—the clatter of tin plates, the scrape of spoons, voices mingling into a rising, falling hum. Fred took comfort in the familiarity of it, the way laughter sparked even in exhaustion, the way men jostled shoulders over a game of cards or passed round a cigarette on deck when the weather allowed.

In those moments, when he let himself lean against the rail with the sea stretching out in all directions, Fred thought of home. He thought of Nancy, her face sharp and clear in his mind, and the small, ordinary life he longed to return to. Out here, survival was not just about evading the enemy—it was about holding on, through fatigue and routine, to the hope that the ocean would one day give him back to her.

Fred leaned against the bulkhead, rolling his shoulders after another long watch. The low rumble of the engines vibrated through the steel, steady as a heartbeat.

"Don't tell me you're planning on standing here all day," came Jack Curzon's voice, gruff but light with amusement. The petty officer had a knack for spotting when a man was running himself thin.

Fred huffed a quiet laugh. "Feels like it. Might as well chain me to the wheel."

Jack raised an eyebrow, jerking his head toward the mess. "Come on. Galley's open. Grab a mug of tea, stretch your legs where the benches are warm. Ship'll manage without you for ten minutes."

Fred shook his head, half smiling. "If I sit down, I'll not get back up."

"That's the point," Jack said dryly. "You don't, and next watch you'll be asleep on your feet. Besides, there's a card game going—might be your lucky day."

Fred hesitated, the thought of the crowded, noisy mess pulling at him. It wasn't comfort, not exactly, but it was something. He pushed away from the bulkhead, falling into step beside Jack.

"Alright," he muttered, a touch of weariness beneath his grin. "But only if you promise not to take all my rations in the pot."

Jack snorted. "No promises, lad. That's half the fun."

They ducked through the low doorway into the mess deck, the buzz of voices and scrape of cutlery wrapping around them at once. The light was dim, the bulbs swaying slightly with the ship's roll, but there was a strange comfort in the bustle—men crowded shoulder to shoulder, mugs in hand, the usual chorus of laughter, grumbles, and clattering tin.

Jack slid onto a bench, patting the space beside him. "See? Not so bad. Bit of noise, bit of warmth. Better than staring at bulkheads."

Fred lowered himself down, stretching his legs under the table. "Can't argue with that." He took the steaming mug handed to him, the warmth seeping into his hands.

Across the table a pair of lads were bent over a battered pack of cards, coins and cigarette rations stacked between them as the pot. Jack nodded toward them with a sly grin. "Told you. Could make a fortune here, if you've the luck."

Fred chuckled. "Or lose a week's smokes in ten minutes. No thanks."

"Always the cautious one," Jack teased, leaning back with his mug. Then his tone softened, more thoughtful. "But you're right. Better to keep what's yours. Never know when you'll need it."

Fred glanced around the mess—the chatter, the clatter, the tired but familiar faces—and let out a breath he hadn't realised he'd been holding. "Suppose that's true of everything these days."

Jack gave him a long, balanced look, then raised his mug. "Aye. Life's just about keeping hold of what you can."

They sat in companionable silence for a moment, the ship rolling gently beneath them, the sound of laughter and cards filling the space between words. For all the weariness of the sea, Fred felt the knot in his chest ease a little. The war was still out there, but here—in the mess, with Jack beside him—it seemed distant, for a while.

The lull was broken when a runner ducked into the mess, his voice carrying over the chatter. "Shore leave's confirmed for tomorrow. First watch gets the morning boat across."

At once the room shifted—the tired hum of conversation flaring into cheers, whistles, and the scrape of benches as men leaned toward each other in sudden excitement. Cards were abandoned, mugs lifted in mock toasts. Someone at the back struck up a half-hearted tune on a mouth organ, and laughter followed.

Jack's grin widened as he tipped his mug toward Fred. "Well, there's your fortune, lad. A night off steel decks and salt spray. Maybe even a pint that isn't watered down."

Fred couldn't help but smile, the thought of solid ground beneath his boots tugging at something deep inside him. "And a proper bed," he added.

Jack chuckled. "Aye, though with your luck, you'll end up on a dockside bunkhouse mattress older than your grandmother."

Fred laughed with him, but the thought of a few hours ashore—of faces that weren't grey with fatigue, of streets that held some echo of home—was enough to fill his chest with a quiet warmth. Shore leave never lasted long, but it was a reminder there was more to life than watches, waves, and war. For the first time in weeks, he let himself feel almost light.

By the next morning, the mood across the ship was lighter, almost buoyant. Men leaned at the rails, squinting toward the faint smudge on the horizon that slowly sharpened into the line of the coast. The grey expanse of sea seemed to brighten as the destroyer ploughed steadily forward, every mile bringing them closer to solid ground.

Fred stood on the foredeck, the wind tugging at his cap, watching rooftops and cranes begin to rise out of the haze. The bustle of the harbour was still distant, but the sight of land—real land—was enough to stir a ripple of chatter along the deck. It was as though the very air had changed, carrying with it the promise of streets, voices, and life beyond the unbroken horizon of the sea. Fred drew a deep breath, feeling the tension in his shoulders ease. Shore was in sight, and for a brief time, war would loosen its grip.

FORGET FOR A LITTLE WHILE

The bunks were narrow, stacked in neat rows, each with a curtain that could be drawn for a measure of privacy. The air was cooler here than in the mess, quieter too, broken only by the soft rustle of pages turning or the low murmur of voices in the half-light. Nancy sat cross-legged on her bed, mending a button on her tunic with quick, careful stitches, while Mary perched opposite, a letter unfolded in her lap.

Mary smoothed the creased paper with her fingertips, her face alight with the mix of pride and worry that only family could bring. "From my brother," she said, lifting the letter slightly as if to prove it. "He's out in Italy now. Says it's hot as blazes and the dust gets into everything—boots, blankets, even his tea."

Nancy paused her stitching, looking up with interest. "And how is he keeping?"

Mary's smile flickered. "He says he's well enough, but you know how they write. Always trying to sound braver than they feel." She tucked a loose strand of hair behind her ear, voice softening. "When he was drafted, I couldn't just sit at home and wait. Joining the Wrens felt like… the least I could do. A way of standing with him, in my own way."

There was a quiet honesty in her tone, and Nancy felt a swell of affection for her friend. She understood that need—to do something, anything, rather than sit by helplessly while the world tore itself apart.

Mary folded the letter again, pressing it to her chest for a moment before slipping it into the pocket of her tunic. "He'd laugh if he saw me now, I think. But I know he'd be proud, too."

Nancy reached across the narrow space, giving her hand a gentle squeeze. "He should be. You're doing your part. We both are."

For a moment, the two of them sat in the soft light of the bunkroom, the whirr of the base distant beyond the walls. In that small, steady space, friendship grew—stitched together not just by duty, but by shared hopes, fears, and the fragile threads of family far away.

Nancy had just knotted off her thread when the door creaked open and in bustled Elsie, cheeks flushed, eyes bright with the kind of energy that always preceded a scrap of gossip.

"You'll never guess," she announced, hands on her hips as half of the room turned to look up from letters and books. "Word's just come down—there's to be a dance tomorrow evening. Music and everything!"

The room shifted at once, the quiet broken by a ripple of laughter and chatter. A few of the girls groaned good-naturedly, already worrying about clean uniforms or borrowed shoes, but most lit up at the thought of music and movement beyond the rhythmic tramp of drills and duties.

Mary's face brightened, and she let out a low whistle. "A dance? Here? Well, that'll give the lads something to fuss over." She turned to Nancy, eyes sparkling. "What do you say? Bit of music might do us good."

Nancy couldn't help but smile at her friend's eagerness. The idea of a dance—of stepping out of routine, even just for an evening—stirred something warm inside her. "I'd say it is certainly not my usual type of thing, but I am sure, it'll be just what we need."

Elsie plopped down on the edge of a nearby bunk, grinning at the stir she'd caused. "Better get yourselves ready, girls. Tomorrow we're not just Wrens—we're belles of the ball."

The room filled with a buzz of excitement, the earlier stillness giving way to a new energy. Letters and sewing were set aside, talk turning instead to dresses tucked away in trunks, who might be asked to dance, and the hope that, for a few hours at least, war could be forgotten in the sway of music and the gleam of polished shoes.

As the chatter swirled around them, Mary leaned closer to Nancy, her voice soft enough to keep the moment between them. "I do love a party," she confessed, her smile touched with a kind of wistful longing. "Back home, before all this, they were my favourite. My mum would fuss with my hair, and there'd always be too much cake and not enough chairs. I can still hear the gramophone crackling in the corner."

Her eyes grew distant for a moment, as though she were seeing it all again—the crowded kitchen, the laughter spilling into the garden, the faint glow of fairy lights strung across a hedge. She gave a small shrug, almost shy. "Feels like another lifetime. It's been years since I've been to anything like that. A proper party, I mean—not just us sneaking a sing-song after lights out."

Nancy smiled at the picture her friend painted, her needle forgotten in her lap. "Well, then tomorrow will be your chance," she said gently. "A proper dance again, even if it's only for an evening."

Mary's grin returned, brighter this time. "Aye, and I'll not waste it. I don't care if I've two left feet—I'll dance to every song if I can."

Nancy laughed softly, warmed by her friend's joy, and in that moment she found herself looking forward to the dance as much as Mary did.

The evening of the dance arrived with a flutter of excitement that spread through the Wrens' quarters like a tide. Trunks were opened, uniforms brushed and pressed, and scraps of borrowed perfume passed from hand to hand with giggles and mock protests.

Mary stood before a small, spotted mirror, carefully tracing a line of lipstick across her mouth. She turned with a triumphant grin and waved the tube at Nancy. "Your turn."

Nancy, sat on the edge of her bunk, shook her head. "Oh, no. Not me. I'll only make a mess of it."

"Don't be daft." Mary hauled her to her feet and tilted her chin, her tone firm but playful. "You'll thank me when the sailors line up for a dance. Trust me—bit of colour never hurt anyone."

Nancy rolled her eyes but held still as Mary carefully dabbed the lipstick on. She pulled back with a laugh. "There. Perfect. See? You look a picture."

"I feel ridiculous," Nancy muttered, though a reluctant smile betrayed her.

Around them, the girls chattered about the evening ahead, voices bubbling with anticipation. Elsie was already plotting who she might catch the eye of, while another pair joked about how long it would take before the sailors grew tipsy on their rationed rum.

"They'll be falling over themselves after a few glasses," Mary said knowingly, slipping her lipstick back into her pocket. "It's the need to forget, isn't it? Forget the sea, forget the danger. Can't say I blame them."

Nancy smoothed her skirt and nodded. "Nor can I. Perhaps tonight we'll all forget, just for a little while."

Mary looped her arm through Nancy's with a sparkle in her eye. "Exactly. So come on, love—we're going to dance like the world isn't falling apart."

Together, they joined the stream of Wrens heading out into the night, laughter echoing down the corridor, their worries tucked away behind polished shoes and borrowed smiles.

NAVAL DANCE

The blackout made even the village hall feel like a secret. Heavy curtains were pinned tight over the windows, the only light coming from a string of bare bulbs strung across the rafters. Someone had tacked bunting to the walls, though it sagged between the nails, its colours dulled by years of dust. The village hall smelled of polish and paraffin heaters, a thin haze of smoke hanging beneath the rafters.

The gramophone wheezed out a tune, scratchy but cheerful, fighting against the hum of conversation and the scuff of boots on the wooden floor. Wrens and sailors crowded the hall, pressed shoulder to shoulder, their uniforms rumpled, their smiles too bright. Everyone was trying — trying to forget the cold sea, the raids, the telegrams that could come at any moment. For a few hours, they wanted music instead of static, laughter instead of sirens.

Nancy stood near the edge of the room, tea mug clutched between her hands. She'd borrowed Mary's lipstick, though it felt odd on her lips, like a costume. She told herself she'd only come to keep Mary company. Her eyes kept straying to the dance floor, where pairs circled awkwardly, trying to pretend they weren't thinking of tomorrow.

A band of sailors cheered too loudly in one corner of the hall, their laughter edged with weariness. Across the room, two Wrens whispered together, heads bent close, sharing gossip Nancy couldn't catch. And above it all, the gramophone needle crackled on, spinning hope into the air.

For a moment, Nancy let herself imagine what it would be like if the world were different — if Edward hadn't been lost to the sea, if Fred Harding's quiet gaze hadn't unsettled her in ways she didn't want to admit. If she were just a girl at a dance, waiting for someone to ask her to take the floor.

This, however, was wartime, and nothing was simple.

She hadn't meant to come tonight. Mary had tugged her arm and insisted — "You need air, Nance. And maybe a dance, if you're lucky."

"Evening."

She started at the voice beside her. Lieutenant Harding — Fred. He looked oddly out of place in his uniform here, tall and solemn among the jumble of sailors and Wrens.

Fred wore his lieutenant's uniform with the quiet authority of a man used to the sea. His double-breasted navy jacket bore the two thin gold rings at the cuff, dulled a little by salt and weather, though still sharply pressed. The brass buttons gleamed where he'd polished them himself, and his cap sat square on his head, the white cover faintly smudged from long days aboard. Beneath the jacket, his trousers were neatly creased, the hems stiff with salt spray, and his black shoes carried the scuffs of steel decks despite every attempt to shine them. He looked every inch the officer — but the faint shadow of exhaustion in his eyes and the roughness of his hands betrayed the truth: the war wore down even those in gold braid.

"Evening," she managed, suddenly fascinated by the scuff marks on the floorboards.

For a moment neither spoke. The gramophone needle hissed. Across the hall, a pair of sailors attempted a jitterbug with more enthusiasm than rhythm, drawing laughter from the crowd.

Fred cleared his throat. "I'm not much for these things," he said. "Noise, crowds. I'd rather be—" He stopped himself, then smiled faintly. "Well. Anywhere else."

Nancy surprised herself by laughing — a short, sharp sound. "I feel the same. I only came because my friend insisted."

Their eyes met then, both of them caught in the admission, and Nancy's chest tightened. She looked away first, sipping her tea though it was getting cold.

After a pause, Fred asked quietly, "Would you… care to dance?"

Her heart lurched. Edward had asked her that once, in another hall, another lifetime. For a moment the memory threatened to crush her. She opened her mouth to refuse. But Fred's expression stopped her — not cocky, not expectant, simply hopeful. Almost shy.

She set the mug down. "All right, but I'm warning you, I've two left feet."

Fred smiled properly then, and the years seemed to fall from his face. "That makes two of us."

On the floor, they moved stiffly at first, awkward in the press of bodies. Nancy felt the heat of his hand against hers, the unfamiliar weight of another person holding her so close. Slowly, the music blurred around them, and for the first time in years she allowed herself the smallest sliver of something she had thought lost forever — the dangerous, aching possibility of happiness.

As the gramophone wheezed out another tune and Fred's hand guided hers in time, Nancy's mind flickered back to the first night she had ever seen him. It had been months ago, another dance, another crowded hall thick with uniforms and laughter that rang too loudly against the shadow of war. He had been across the dance floor then — tall, fair-haired, his uniform immaculate, his gaze certain in a way that unsettled her.

They hadn't spoken more than a handful of words. He had been pulled away by friends, she couldn't remember which, and she had thought nothing would come of it. At the end of the night, as she slipped on her coat, she had found herself holding a folded scrap of paper he had left behind. A note, scrawled quickly, almost carelessly, yet enough to set her heart racing.

She hadn't known him then — not really. Just a stranger in a crowded room. However, now, as his palm pressed lightly against her back and his eyes met hers across the sway of the dance, she realised that single, cheeky gesture had been the first thread of something she had never expected to find again.

"Careful, you're stepping on my foot again." Fred said quietly, with a faint smile.

"Oh! I'm sorry, I told you I've two left feet." Nancy flustered.

"Well, that makes four between us. It's a miracle we haven't taken out the entire front row." He teased, smiling into her eyes.

"Perhaps we should warn them to keep a safe distance. Clear the hall, really, for public safety." She relaxed a little.

"Excellent idea. Issue a warning: Lieutenant Harding and Miss Carter are attempting a dance manoeuvre. Approach at your own risk."

Nancy grinned despite herself "That might be the first naval order I've ever agreed with."

They stumbled again, both laughing this time. Fred steadied her gently, his hand lingering at her back.

"Don't worry, Nance. We're terrible. But I'd rather stumble through this with you than glide with anyone else." He said softly, and Nancy felt like they were the only two people in the room.

The night air was sharp after the heat of the dance hall, her breath turning to mist as she and Mary walked back toward the barracks. Their shoes clicked on the cobbles, the blackout making the lane between the huts and buildings feel like a tunnel.

Mary was chattering, replaying every song, every step with the sailor who'd asked her to dance three times. Nancy barely heard her. She still felt the weight of Fred's hand against hers, the awkward rhythm they had found together, the way he had smiled as if it was the first time in weeks he had remembered how. Nancy had willed time to slow down, so that she could enjoy the smiles and the feeling a little longer.

She pressed her coat tighter around her, fighting the warmth rising in her cheeks. Foolish, she told herself. Dangerous. She had promised never again. Still, as Mary laughed beside her, Nancy let herself glance up at the starlit sky and wandered if Fred was thinking of her too.

ONLY A WALK, ONLY A MORNING

Fred rose with the first call of the bosun's pipe, the ship alive again with the clang of hatches and the smell of oil and salt. The night ashore felt like a dream now — the music, the laughter, the girl with quiet eyes who had surprised him with a smile.

As he shaved in the cramped washroom, the other officers joked about the dance, about the drinks and the girls and the gramophone that had skipped half its records. Fred said nothing, just worked the razor slowly across his jaw.

But he saw her still. Nancy. The way she had looked down at her shoes before saying yes, the way she had laughed at herself when she stumbled, the way she had looked up at him once, just once, as though she wasn't afraid to let him in.

The church bells were muffled under the blackout drapes, but their notes carried out into the crisp Sunday air all the same. The congregation spilled slowly from the stone doorway, Wrens in their dark uniforms, sailors in blues, villagers in their best coats. The war had changed everything, but the rhythm of Sunday mornings still held.

Nancy stepped into the sunlight, smoothing her gloves over her fingers. Mary had darted ahead to greet a group of friends, leaving Nancy in the crowd. She turned toward the barracks path — and stopped.

Fred Harding was waiting just beyond the church gate.

He stood a little awkwardly, cap under his arm, his broad shoulders stiff against the low wall. For a moment she thought he hadn't seen her — but then his eyes lifted, and his expression softened.

"Miss Carter," he said, his voice gentler than she remembered from the dance.

"Lieutenant Harding," she replied, too formal, her heart thudding. She adjusted her scarf though it didn't need it.

He hesitated, then smiled faintly. "Fred, if you don't mind. Too formal. After last night, it seems... strange to be so proper."

Nancy couldn't help it — she smiled too, small and careful. "Then Nancy."

They stood for a moment, the chatter of the crowd drifting past, the gulls crying overhead. Fred cleared his throat. "I don't have to sail today. First Sunday in months. Thought I might walk into the village. Get away from the docks for an hour."

Nancy tilted her head. "So, you thought you'd loiter by the churchyard wall in the hope of conscripting a companion?"

His smile widened, crooked and boyish. "Something like that."

For a moment she considered refusing. It would be safer, easier. Then she thought of the dance — the awkward warmth of his hand in hers, the way the music had seemed to play just for them — and heard herself say: "All right, but I'm warning you, I walk faster than I dance."

He laughed, the sound warming the chill air. Together they fell into step, their shoulders almost brushing as they left the churchyard behind.

Nancy tried to tell herself it was only a walk, only a morning. Nothing more. As Fred glanced at her sidelong, as if memorising her face, she felt the fragile flicker of something she thought she'd buried with the loss of Edward: hope.

The lane wound gently away from the churchyard, lined with stone walls and hedgerows glistening with dew. Their footsteps crunched on the gravel, the air bright but cool.

Fred broke the silence first. "So — forgive me prying — but what did you do before all this?" He gestured vaguely, meaning the uniforms, the war, the constant grey of duty.

Nancy smiled faintly. "I worked in a grocer's. Nothing glamorous. Weighed out sugar, wrapped butter, minded the till."

He looked at her, one brow raised. "You? Behind a counter, handing out rashers of bacon?"

She laughed, surprising herself. "Why not me? Someone has to."

"True," Fred conceded, grinning. "Though I can't quite picture it. You seem too… sharp-eyed. Like you'd catch a thief before he even thought about stealing an apple."

Fred weighed the calm steadiness in her eyes. There was a smartness about her — not the sharp edges of ambition, but an intelligence that seemed to weigh and measure everything around her. She carried herself with quiet composure, so much more than the simple shop girl she had once been. Nevertheless, he wandered what that life had been like for her, before uniforms and static-filled headphones, before telegrams and loss had pressed the softness from her. He pictured her behind a grocer's counter, wrapping butter in paper, her hair escaping its pins as she laughed with customers, her world smaller but perhaps gentler. The war had hardened her, yes, but beneath it Fred glimpsed the truth — she had been made for peace, for quiet mornings and simple joys. God help him, he wanted to see her find them again.

Nancy tilted her head, teasing. "And what about you? Did you always plan to be in the Navy?"

Fred hesitated, then gave a wry smile. "Not always. At school, I was hopeless at sums, worse at Latin. But I could lose myself in books. Stories."

Her eyes lit a little. "Fiction?"

He nodded. "Jules Verne, mostly. Twenty Thousand Leagues Under the Sea. Captain Nemo in his Nautilus — I read it cover to cover until the pages nearly fell out. The idea of a ship that could take you anywhere, into the very heart of the sea…" He gave a small shrug, almost embarrassed. "I suppose that's what set me on this course. Seemed nobler than staying in my father's warehouse."

Nancy slowed, her gaze thoughtful. "I loved that book, too. The adventure of it — the danger, the mystery. Though Nemo frightened me a little. So clever, but so cut off, so… lonely."

Fred glanced at her, surprised. "Yes. That's exactly it. He was brilliant, but he carried his grief with him into the depths. Never let it go."

For a moment, Nancy said nothing. Nancy felt tense as a sudden flood of memories came back –

Edward. Lost at sea. The crunch of their boots on the path filled the silence.

Fred seemed to sense the shift. His voice softened. "I used to dream of being like him — master of my own vessel, untouchable. But the truth is… out here, we're nothing without the men beside us. And without someone to come back to."

Nancy met his eyes, her throat tight. She wanted to say something — about Edward, about fear, about how dangerous it felt to be seen like this. Instead she managed a small smile. "I'd have guessed you for a Dickens man. Or Kipling."

Fred chuckled. "Oh, I read those too. But Nemo was the one who got under my skin."

They walked on, the silence between them different now — not awkward, but charged, threaded with something fragile and unspoken.

Nancy and Fred walked slowly up the cobbled street, the morning air cool and sharp with the scent of the sea. The village was only just beginning to stir—shop doors remained closed, their front windows still veiled with pinned blackout curtains, the neat folds catching the pale shafts of daylight that slipped between them. A milk cart rattled distantly, its wheels clattering on the stones, and a gull wheeled overhead, its cry echoing across the harbour.

The clock tower stood watch above the rooftops, its hands glinting faintly in the slanting light. It chimed the half-hour, the sound carrying clear across the water, mingling with the muted slap of tide against the harbour wall. Fred glanced toward it as they passed, but Nancy's gaze lingered—there was something reassuring about its constant presence, as if time itself carried on unshaken, no matter the uncertainty around them.

Ahead, the small tea shop was beginning to open, a curl of smoke rising from its chimney, and the promise of warmth and a quiet pot of tea drew them on.

The tea shop was small and warm, tucked behind the harbour road, its windows steamed from the kettles always on the boil. The blackout curtains were still pinned up from the night before, letting a sliver of grey daylight spill across the tables, highlighting the dust motes in the sunbeam.

Nancy slipped off her gloves, smoothing them flat on her lap as Fred held the chair for her. She felt oddly self-conscious, as if the other customers might be watching. Most of them were doing the same — Wrens with their mugs, sailors hunched over rationed scones, all seizing what scraps of normality they could.

The waitress set down two chipped cups of tea. Fred poured, his big hands surprisingly careful with the pot. "There we are," he said, pushing one cup toward her.

Nancy wrapped her fingers around the china, grateful for the warmth. For a moment neither of them spoke. The quiet stretched, filled only by the clink of crockery and the distant whistle of a kettle.

Fred broke it first. "You said you liked Nemo. Was that your favourite story?"

Nancy smiled faintly. "When I was younger, yes. But I think I liked the idea of escape more than the adventure itself. A world apart from this one. Somewhere safe."

Fred nodded, thoughtful. "That's what I wanted too. But the sea… it's no escape. Not really. It takes as much as it gives."

Nancy looked down at her tea, her chest tightening. Edward. The way his name was carved on the memorial. The telegram folded in her drawer. His voice lost forever to the Atlantic.

Her throat felt dry, but she forced herself to speak. "I lost someone, early in the war. He was at sea." She stopped there, unable to say more, the words snagging against the grief she still carried.

Fred didn't press. He only set his cup down gently, his gaze steady, kind. "I'm sorry."

The simplicity of it undid her. No hollow reassurances, no forced change of subject. Just recognition.

Nancy managed a small nod, blinking quickly. "That's why I shouldn't be here," she murmured, half to herself. "Why I shouldn't… with you."

For a moment, silence again. Then Fred leaned forward, his voice low but firm. "Nancy, if there's one thing I've learned out there, it's that tomorrow isn't promised. Not for me, not for you. All we have is today."

Her heart gave a painful, hopeful twist. She couldn't answer him, not yet. When she lifted her cup again, her hands weren't shaking quite so much.

With Fred, there was a steadiness she had never known before — a quiet reassurance that wrapped around her like a shield. It wasn't just his uniform or his rank; it was the way he looked at her, as though she were safe in his presence, as though the war and all its shadows could not touch her while he stood near. The comfort unsettled her almost as much as it soothed, for she was unaccustomed to leaning on anyone. With Fred, she found herself wanting to.

⚓

Nancy watched him go, his figure shrinking against the bustle of the quay, and felt the old fear press in. She had promised herself never to love a man the sea could take — yet here she was, praying the ocean would be kind enough to give him back.

From the destroyer's deck, Fred glanced back once at the dwindling shore, the village no more than a smudge against the grey horizon. He carried the memory of Nancy's smile like a compass point in his chest — fragile, fleeting, yet enough to steer him through whatever the sea held next.

The sea waited, and the wolves with it. Then as the destroyer slipped her moorings late on that evening, Fred tucked the memory of that dance, and that walk, somewhere deep inside — something worth carrying into the dark.

DARK NIGHTS SEEM LIGHTER

Nancy sat at her desk, the coded slip of paper lying untouched beneath her hand. The room was quiet now, the night shift thinned to only a handful of Wrens bent over their stations. Somewhere, the wireless hummed and cracked with static, but she could not bring herself to lean into it again. Not just yet.

Her thoughts wouldn't leave Fred Harding alone. The way he'd looked at her at the dance — steady, almost shy, as if he'd rather have been back on his ship than standing under a blackout lamp in a village hall. She'd caught herself smiling when she thought of it, and that terrified her.

Because she had smiled like that before. With Edward.

Edward had been all confidence and laughter, filling the room so completely she'd thought nothing could touch him. They had walked by the river only a few short weeks before his posting, planning a future in fragments — a cottage, a garden, a dog. She could still hear his voice if she closed her eyes, teasing her about her "sensible shoes" and the way she wrinkled her nose when she concentrated. Then the telegram had arrived. Early in the war. No grave to visit, only a name carved into stone.

She pressed her hands flat against the desk, grounding herself. That part of her heart was supposed to be sealed. Untouchable.

Nancy forced herself to focus on the paper before her, as she took up her pencil to start scratching as she worked through the cipher, she reached her hand into the pocket to thumb the note Fred had left her the first time they had met, many months ago, still it was neatly folded and safely kept in her pocket. Duty first. Always. Yet, in the silence of the signal room, she allowed herself a whispered distraction:

Was it betrayal to hope again?

The thought was soon followed by the note, in her pocket: *You make the dark nights seem lighter.* A flicker of a smile appeared, fleeting on Nancy's face. Before her concentration and determination resumed.

As Nancy regathered her focus, she turned to the next slip, and noticed a smudge of thick ink across a piece of code. How could this happen, Nancy thought to herself. She held the slip up to the dim light, to see if it would help. Nothing. The blotted ink had completely ruined the scribe.

Nancy lowered her pencil, staring at the string of numbers she had tried to review. Somewhere out in the Atlantic, a destroyer's captain would be reading the same figures, making the same calculations. Would their codes be right? Perhaps it was Fred.

As quickly as the thought came, it left Nancy's mind—distracted by a sudden movement towards the corridor. Harvey, one of the senior officers, scurried out of the signals room, his arms laden with a stack of papers clutched almost too tightly to his chest. He moved briskly, his eyes fixed ahead, barely acknowledging anyone he passed. For a moment Nancy frowned, her pencil paused above the paper. It was unusual—odd, even—to see him like that. Officers didn't usually fetch and carry for themselves, certainly not in such a hurry.

She watched as he disappeared around the corner, the echo of his footsteps fading down the passage. The image stayed with her, though she couldn't have said why: the stiff set of his shoulders, the way he hugged the papers close, as though shielding them from sight. A prickling sense of unease tugged at her, a whisper that something was stirring beneath the ordinary routine. She shook her head, forcing her attention back to her work. Still, the thought lingered—it was strange behaviour. Strange enough to make her wonder.

Nancy glanced around the room to see if anyone else had noticed. Elsie's eyes were fixed on the doorway to the corridor, but the moment she caught Nancy watching, she dropped her gaze and busied herself with her work as if nothing at all were out of place.

⚓

The Atlantic stretched endless and grey in every direction, the horizon blurred by drizzle and low cloud. The convoy plodded onward, thirty ships in a slow, stubborn line, their wakes fanning out like white scars across the water. Smoke from their funnels smeared the sky, a signal for every U-boat within a hundred miles.

Fred stood on the bridge of the destroyer. The ship's hull shuddered with every wave, spray lashing across the deck in sheets. Below him, the men moved about their duties with weary precision — a lookout stamping his feet for warmth, a signalman tugging his scarf tighter, a stoker pausing to cough into his sleeve.

Convoy duty was monotonous until it wasn't. Hours of staring into endless grey, punctuated by minutes of terror when the wolves struck. Fred knew that routine too well, and so did his men. He saw it in their eyes — the mixture of boredom and dread. A few joked, swapping cigarettes, their laughter carried away by the wind. Others stayed silent, watching the freighters as though willing them to stay afloat.

The wireless operator brought up a slip of paper, damp from the mist. Fred scanned it quickly — position reports, coded chatter. Nothing unusual. Still, he tucked it into his pocket, his jaw tightening. The sea was too quiet. The wolves were out there, waiting.

He drew in a slow breath and let it out, forcing the knot in his chest to ease. His mind slipped, unbidden, to the shore. To the village hall strung with bunting, to the gramophone's crackle, to the feel of Nancy's hand in his at the dance, and to that morning after, the walk and the tea shop, the way her smile had flickered when she let herself laugh.

Fred almost chuckled at the thought of it. The note he'd left her, months ago, had been little more than cheek then — *You make the dark nights seem lighter.* He hadn't known her, not really. It had been a sailor's flourish, nothing more.

Out here with the grey pressing down and the Atlantic yawning endless beneath him, he realised he had meant more than he knew. She was the thought he carried into the dark, the small flame against the endless night.

Fred watched the life of the ship unfold beneath him. The destroyer moved like a living thing, every man a pulse within it. Sailors hurried along the deck with ropes coiled over their shoulders, their boots striking sharp against the steel. Signalmen clattered up the ladder to the bridge wing, flags snapping into the breeze, their hands deft and practised. At the aft, a gunnery crew swung their weapon into position with brisk precision, their faces set with the concentration of men who had drilled this movement a hundred times.

There was urgency in every step, yet no chaos. Each man knew his place, his part, and together they wove the rhythm that kept *Fury* alive. Fred leaned on the steel bulk, his gaze sweeping over them, pride and worry twisting together in his chest. These were boys, many of them still teenagers, yet in their hands lay the safety of the convoy, the lives of countless men beyond their sight. The ship relied on them, and they relied on him. That knowledge weighed heavy, but it also steadied him. He would not let them falter. Not while he had breath left in him.

A shout from the lookout snapped him back. "Smoke on the horizon!"

Fred straightened, his voice firm as he barked the order to bring her about. The destroyer surged forward, her bow cutting into the swell, the men at their stations again, nerves taut as wires.

The convoy steamed on, the sea stretching bleak and endless. Fred braced himself, holding to that quiet truth: whatever the ocean took, it hadn't yet taken him from Nancy.

The destroyer pitched hard to starboard, sending spray lashing across the bridge windows. Fred held onto the rail with one hand, grounding himself as the officer of the watch, before he barked a course correction. Another night, another stretch of cold black ocean, the convoy steaming slow and heavy ahead.

He should have been thinking only of bearings, fuel consumption, the curve of the radar trace. But his mind wandered, treacherously, to Scotland. To the Wren with watchful eyes who seemed to carry the weight of the war in her silence.

Nancy.

Nancy carried an air of composure that belied her years. Her face was youthful still, the kind that revealed more softness in quiet moments than she ever allowed on duty. Blonde hair, waved and pinned back with precise neatness, framed her features, though in the damp air of the base a few strands always slipped free against her temples. Her eyes were a cold, clear blue — watchful, steady, the sort that could make even seasoned officers hesitate when she fixed them in place. Yet when she smiled, the severity melted away, her whole expression brightening as if she had opened a window to let in the sun. It was a smile that lit a room, a smile that made men stop mid-sentence and women glance up from their work, for in that moment she seemed untouchable by the war that shadowed them all.

The sonar operator broke his thoughts.

"Sir — faint contact, bearing green eighty. Could be drift, could be a boat."

Fred leaned forward, scanning the darkness beyond the bow. Nothing but the pulsing thrum of the engines and the ghosts of waves under starlight. Still, his pulse quickened. U-boats were never far.

"Maintain course," he ordered evenly. "But keep your ears sharp."

The operator nodded. The men needed his calm, his certainty. He'd learned long ago that command was less about orders and more about steadiness. Even when inside, the doubts gnawed like rats.

He exhaled into the night, pulling his collar tighter. Somewhere beyond this endless sea, Nancy would be at her desk, pencil in hand, listening for the enemy in the static. She was part of the same battle, just fighting from another front. The thought steadied him more than any compass could.

For a fleeting moment, he allowed himself the luxury of a picture: walking with her along a riverbank, spring light instead of blackout shadows. Something worth coming back for.

Fred's mind diverted to another thought. The thought of home and his friends – Harry, a fellow naval comrade, stationed in the Mediterranean, and Harold, a private in the army – Fred closed his eyes and flashed a subtle smile at the thought of Harry based in the Mediterranean, his thoughts told him he must be warmer than he currently was, then swiftly he wandered, where Harold might be, and hoped that they were both safe.

Fred startled as once again his thoughts were interrupted, the signal bell clanged sharp and urgent. Another contact. The wolves were close tonight.

MY DEAREST…

The world was quiet, Nancy sat in the mess with Mary, Elsie, and the other Wrens, after they had finished eating their evening meal of hot vegetable soup and rationed sourdough bread.

The air thick with coal smoke and the faint smell of soup. Nancy, Mary and Elsie sat shoulder to shoulder at a long wooden table, empty bowls pushed aside.

"If I never see another bowl of vegetable soup, it'll be too soon. I swear I'm half turnip by now." Mary groaned, not ungrateful for being fed, but out of sheer monotony.

"It wasn't so bad. At least it was hot." Nancy chirped in, looking at Elsie, slumped against the table.

"Hot, yes. Tasty? No. One day, I'll smuggle in real sausages. We'll have a feast. You'll both thank me." Mary beamed at Nancy and Elsie, the thought of sausages bringing her to life.

"And when the Commander asks where you got them, shall I tell him to look for a trail of breadcrumbs back to the pig farm?" Without missing a beat, Elsie chirped in, dryly.

"You wound me, Elsie. Do you think me capable of petty theft?" Mary reacted with a mocking gasp, clutching her hands to her chest.

"Capable and likely." Nancy teased.

"Nance? You're meant to be on my side!" Mary laughed, nudging Nancy in the ribs.

"Enough nonsense, you two. We work hard, and the least we can do is be grateful for a hot meal. Some men out there would give anything for this soup, turnips and all." Elsie replied, her tone firm, but fair, as with everything Elsie said, or did.

Mary lowered her eyes, chastened but still grinning. For a moment, the laughter faded, replaced by quiet understanding. Mary broke the silence, lifting her empty mug of tea, like a toast: "To the Navy: may it serve us something other than soup before the war is over."

"You're impossible, Mary." Elsie said shaking her head, unable to hide her smile.

The conversation abruptly ended with the arrival of post, letters were distributed to the recipients. Nancy's eyes lit up when handed a small cream envelope addressed to *'Miss Carter'*. Nancy knew the writing.

My Dearest Nancy,

The sea is black tonight, the kind of black that swallows even the stars. The only light comes from the faint glow of our funnels and the phosphorescence in the waves — ghostly trails in the dark. I should be sleeping, but I find my thoughts drift to you, and so I take up my pencil instead.

It seems mad, doesn't it? To have known you only a handful of days ashore, and yet to feel as though you've lodged yourself in the very heart of me. I keep thinking back to that morning walk, the way you laughed when I admitted Captain Nemo was my boyhood hero. I have been in ships for years,

Nancy, but in all that time I never felt so anchored as I did walking beside you.

The men here joke and sing to keep their spirits up. I do the same, outwardly. But there are moments — after the guns fall silent, or when the horizon is too still — when fear seeps in. It is then I remember your smile, and it steadies me. You make the dark nights seem lighter, more than I ever realised when I scrawled that silly note. I mean it now with all I have.

If I could, I'd promise you safety, that I will return unchanged, untouched. However, I will say, the sea allows no promises. All I can vow is this: that wherever I am, in the roar of the Atlantic or the silence of the watch, I am yours. Entirely, hopelessly yours.

Yours always,

Fred

Nancy felt her eyes well. She stood abruptly, darting from the mess hall, leaving her friends sat in bewilderment. "Nance" she heard Mary shout after her "Nance is everything alright." Mary's voice faded to nothing as she clattered past Commander Talbot and Commander Harvey heading into the mess hall, and left the door swinging behind her.

Nancy re-read the letter three times, the paper softening under her fingers where she traced his words. Each line carried his voice, comforting and warm even across the miles of sea between them, it made her chest ache with something she dared not name. Fred's promise was no promise at all — *the sea allows no promises* — yet his vow of being hers was more than Edward had ever had the chance to give. That thought both shamed and steadied her. She pressed the letter to her lips, her throat tight, torn between the instinct to guard her heart and the undeniable pull of hope. For the first time since Edward's name was carved into stone, she let herself imagine a future that wasn't only loss.

Decidedly Nancy headed towards her bunk. Grabbing a pencil to respond to Fred. She knew where he was headed, so could get a letter to await his arrival.

Dear Fred,

Your letter reached me this evening, and I hardly know what to say. It feels strange to read such warmth written to me, when the world around us allows so little of it. I spend my days listening to voices in the static, none of which I can ever answer. Perhaps that is why your words struck me so — they were not static, but clear, certain, and meant for me alone.

I ought to be sensible. You and I both know how uncertain things are, how quickly the sea can claim what we hold dear. Yet, when I read that I make the dark nights lighter, I found myself smiling like a fool. I keep telling myself not to, but there it is.

You know — I lost someone before, early in the war. His name is on a memorial now, and there are days when I feel I walk in his shadow. It makes me afraid, Fred. Afraid of caring again, of standing at another graveside. When I think of you, of the way you look at me as though I am worth seeing, something inside me refuses to be afraid.

So please, be careful at sea. If you do find yourself thinking of me in the dark hours, know that I am thinking of you too, always — even with pencil in hand, headphones pressed tight, waiting for the dawn.

Yours,

Nancy

Only a few short weeks later, another letter arrived, again a small cream envelope, surprisingly crisp for the miles she considered it had travelled.

My Dearest Nancy,

I read your letter under the dimmest of lights, huddled in the corner of the bridge while the ship creaked and shuddered beneath me. I must have read it a dozen times since. You wrote that my words were not static, but clear and meant for you alone. I can't tell you how much that means — for there are so many things I wish I could say aloud but must trust to ink instead.

You spoke of the one you lost. Edward. I am sorry, truly, and I won't pretend to understand what it cost you. But let me say this: nothing I feel for you takes his place, nor should it. What you had with him was real and true, and no one can take that from you. Nancy — that doesn't mean there isn't room for something new, something different, something ours.

Out here, in the black hours when the sea groans and the men sleep uneasily in their hammocks, I think of you. Not as a shadow behind me, but as a light ahead. Whatever the sea decides, it can't take that from me.

Be proud of your courage, Nance. You carry more strength than you see. If I can carry even a fragment of your hope with me on these nights, then I am the luckiest man afloat.

Until I am back on solid ground,

Yours always,

Fred

This time, Nancy didn't feel a swell of conflicting emotions, just happiness as she read the words on the paper in her hands.

Nancy closed her eyes in the wireless hut, letting the static fade into the background for just a moment. She pictured Fred's smile — crooked, unguarded — and imagined what it would be like to see it not across a crowded dance floor or in hurried snatches of leave, but across a breakfast table on a quiet morning, with no sirens, no convoys, no fear. The thought was so ordinary, so impossible, and yet it filled her chest with a warmth the war could not touch.

Then the thought hit Nancy: how can Fred find the time to write. She smiled subtly to herself at the thought of him stealing time to write her letters.

After her shift, before she went to sleep that night, Nancy sat, pencil in hand writing back to Fred by candle light, as he had read her previous letter.

Dearest Fred,

Your last letter arrived yesterday, and I read it by lamplight until the words nearly blurred. You'll laugh, but I tucked it into my pocket when I went on watch, as though keeping it close would steady my hand on the pencil. It worked, too — my logs were the neatest they've ever been.

The days are lengthening now. We walked to the village yesterday evening, and the hills were soft with spring. I found myself wondering what you'd make of them, whether you'd complain of the climb or race to the top just to prove a point. Somehow, I think it would be the latter.

I won't say more than I should, but I'll say this: you've given me something to look forward to, and that's no small thing in times like these.

Take care of yourself, Fred, and when the sea grows dark, remember there's someone ashore who thinks of you and finds the night a little lighter for it.

Yours,

Nancy

THE LINE DIED

The signals hut was cold enough to see her breath. A single paraffin stove spluttered in the corner, filling the air with the scent of paraffin, but failing to fight the draught that crept beneath the door. Nancy flexed her fingers, rubbed them together, then returned to her headphones. The wireless hissed, all static and scraps of voices, like ghosts lost in the ether.

The windows were fogged at the corners despite the chill, and condensation dripped steadily down, blurring the view of the harbour outside. Inside, the low hum of equipment never stopped—static rasping, dials clicking, the staccato crackle of Morse filling the air like the tapping of restless fingers.

Wrens bent over their desks, headphones pressed tight, pencils scratching furiously in neat columns. The world beyond those thin walls seemed distant, unreal; here, the war reduced itself to bursts of sound and symbols, messages half-heard but heavy with consequence.

Most nights the monotony numbed her. Tonight, however, something was different.

"…Convoy… bearing 221… request—"

The words dissolved into static. Nancy leaned forward, pencil poised. The voice was distant, strained, cut off mid-sentence. Her pulse quickened. She scribbled the fragments on the pad in front of her, passing the sheet down the line to the duty officer. He gave a sharp nod, already reaching for the red phone.

She tried to breathe, tried to focus. Her thoughts seemed to dart elsewhere. Fred was at sea. *Was it his convoy? Was it his voice that had broken through the static?*

Mary nudged her elbow gently, murmuring, "You're pale as milk, Nance. Are you all right?"

Nancy nodded stiffly, eyes fixed on the receiver. Another burst of static, then the faint drone of an engine picked up in the background of the transmission. After seconds, which felt like a lifetime of the engine droning, sound—clear, urgent words:

"Under attack—U-boats—position—"

The line died.

For a moment the hut was frozen. Only the hiss of the radio remained. Nancy realised she was gripping the edge of the desk so hard her knuckles ached. She forced her fingers to relax, though her chest was tight with dread.

"Right," the officer barked, snapping the room into motion. "Get this passed to command. Now."

Mary dashed off with the signal. All around them, typewriters clattered, runners burst in and out with urgent papers, the little hut suddenly a hive of activity.

Nancy sat very still, headphones pressed to her ears, heart pounding. She strained for another voice, another scrap of sound, anything to tell her that Fred — wherever he was — was alive.

The wireless only hissed, empty and merciless.

Nancy pressed the headphones tighter against her ears, her pencil poised uselessly above the logbook. Static hissed and crackled, an endless, mocking monotony that gnawed at her nerves. She willed it to break, to spark, to carry *anything* across the void — a burst of German chatter, a convoy report, even a misfired signal — anything that proved the world beyond the hut was still moving, still alive. The silence was worse than noise; silence meant waiting, imagining, fearing. She leaned forward, eyes fixed on the dials as though she could summon the voices herself, her breath catching with every flicker, her heart aching for the relief of sound.

⚓

Far out on the Atlantic, the sea reared and rolled beneath HMS *Fury* as though intent on testing her resolve. The decks were slick with spray, boots thundering as sailors moved to their stations. Orders barked into the wind vanished almost instantly, yet every man seemed to know his role by instinct, each action rehearsed a hundred times before. Fred gripped the rail as the ship pitched, his gaze fixed on the grey horizon where the convoy straggled ahead. Their safety depended on vigilance, on never letting the sea—or the enemy—catch them unawares. He allowed himself only the briefest thought of Nancy, safe onshore, before returning his mind to the immediate, brutal business of survival.

The night was ink-black, the sea a rolling wall that swallowed the horizon. Fred balanced as the destroyer heaved, spray lashing his face, the wind biting through wool and oilskin alike. Somewhere out in the dark, the convoy ploughed on — hulking merchantmen heavy with supplies — and somewhere closer still, the U-boats waited.

The first torpedo struck just before midnight.

The wail of the klaxon deafening across the ships. Within seconds, the eerie silence of the Atlantic had turned into an ear piercing, heart stopping sound of hell.

A dull, sickening boom tore through the air, followed by the shriek of men and the groan of steel splitting apart. Fred's stomach lurched. Flames leapt into the night, painting the waves orange. One of the tankers had been hit — she was already breaking in two.

"Hard a 'starboard!" the order rang, but Fred hardly heard it. His eyes were fixed on the water. Figures were thrashing in the oil-slick sea, their cries thin against the roar of fire. He wanted to leap in, to pull them all out with his bare hands. But… he couldn't. They had to keep moving. The convoy depended on it.

The guns opened up, the deafening bark of depth charges dropped over the stern. With every drop the destroyer rumbled, trembled, as did the men aboard. The sea boiled with fury, black waves surging.

The destroyer shuddered from the blast of depth charges. Smoke stinging the air. Fred stabilised himself at the rail, eyes fixed on the convoy ahead. A boy no older than eighteen — his face pale, hands trembling — glanced up to Fred, horrified.

"Are we… are we going to make it, sir?" the low voice said.

Fred heard the breaking in his voice, and met his eyes, "Yes. We'll make it. Keep your post — the convoy needs you." Fred kept his voice calm and steady, even though he could feel his heart hammering away within his chest.

The boy didn't verbally respond, a single, simple nod of defiance, swallowing hard, he gripped his station tighter. Fred turned back to the black sea, hiding the weight of the promise he just made.

For an hour, the destroyer danced between life and death, engines straining, the crew running, shouting, firing blind into the night.

Just as suddenly as it had begun, the ocean fell back to the unnerving yet familiar silence. The burning tanker was sinking fast, her bow vanishing beneath the waves. The men in the water… there were fewer now. Too few.

Fred's hands shook as he lit a cigarette, though it did nothing to warm him. The bitter smoke stung his eyes. He thought of the men he had shared tea with only earlier that week, before the convoy set off, men now swallowed by the Atlantic. Their laughter gone, their mugs still cooling in the mess.

He felt an unfriendly weight in his chest, heavier than any sea. Why?

The question gnawed at him, worse than the cold. He knew it would follow him long after the flames died out.

Beneath it all, another thought pressed, unspoken but relentless:

If I don't make it home, Nancy will never know.

Fred, filled with grief, desperate abhorrence, for the war, the axis forces, the killing machines that were stalking them, hunting them each day, stormed into the bridge. Slamming the door behind him. Slamming his fists against his desk. Cold sweat, from fear, from stress formed on his brow. This was the first time the calm, collected, steady under-fire Lieutenant Fred Harding had shown such distressed emotion.

The calm re-gathered. Fred collected himself. Expelling his fury. The only thing he felt he needed to do, was write to Nancy. He couldn't shake thoughts of her from his mind.

Nancy,

There are things I want to say that no envelope should ever carry. Out here, the sea swallows everything — men, ships, words — and I fear that if I send this, it will never reach you, or worse, that it will and I'll sound like a fool.

I'm afraid, Nance. Not of dying — not exactly — but of not seeing you again. Of slipping under one night and leaving nothing but oil on the surface, and you never knowing that I thought of you with my last breath.

I have lost count of how many times I've whispered your name in the dark, when the ship is quiet and only the screws turn. You're the one constant thing in my head, the one light that cuts through the black Atlantic.

If the sea takes me, promise me you'll keep living. Don't let it chain you as it has so many others. You deserve mornings filled with laughter, not silence.

I love you. I've no right to write it, not with so little time between us, but it's the truest thing I know.

— F.

He never signed it. The paper was torn in half the next morning, stuffed into the stove before the first watch.

Fred didn't sleep. He wrestled with the thought instead. He lay in his bunk, boots still on, staring at the steel above his head. The ship creaked and groaned with the swell; every sound magnified in the silence that followed battle. He could still see the tanker's death — the orange bloom of fire, the men flailing in burning water — every time he shut his eyes. The others had dropped into uneasy sleep, worn out by adrenaline and fear, but rest wouldn't come for him. He felt the weight of command pressing on his chest, heavier than the blanket. He'd given the right orders, done all that could be done, and yet the smell of smoke lingered in his nose, accusing. The wolves had struck again, and he was still alive when so many weren't.

Fred turned on his side, pressing his fist against his mouth to stifle the groan that rose in his throat. He should have felt relief — his ship was intact, his men alive — but all he could taste was bitterness. Why them and not us? Why had fate spared his destroyer while the tanker burned, while men clawed at the waves until the sea closed over them? He told himself he had done his duty, that no captain could save everyone, but the truth gnawed at him in the dark. He was breathing, and they were not.

That, he thought bleakly, was the cruelest burden of all.

Fred wanted nothing more than to be home, to be safe, away from the war. He thought of land and he thought of home, and then the first word that came to mind when he thought about it all…

He whispered Nancy's name under his breath, unheard over the engines. Hundreds of miles away, in the stillness of the signal hut, Nancy lifted her head as though she'd been called.

⚓

Back on land, the sound of aircraft droned faintly overhead, a constant reminder of vulnerability. Even in moments of pause, war pressed in from every side: ration books checked at the bakery, blackout curtains pulled taut against the dusk, the muffled rumble of a convoy heading out to sea. For Nancy and Mary, laughter was their rebellion against it all—stolen fragments of joy between duty shifts, as if daring the world to remember there was life worth living beyond the war.

The room was close, thick with the smell of hot valves, dust and damp. Nancy raised her head from her set momentarily before pressing on, knuckles white around her pencil, her ears straining for every crackle of sound. The others worked steadily, passing slips back and forth, but her pulse hammered so loud she could barely hear the static. Somewhere out there, Fred's convoy was in the dark, and she had no way of knowing if he was alive or already claimed by the sea.

The hiss snapped, jagged, as if the air itself had cracked open. Nancy jolted upright, heart leaping, pencil flying across the page before she'd even registered the words. A harsh burst of German filled her ears, broken, urgent, tumbling over itself in clipped syllables. She scribbled furiously, her pulse racing with the suddenness of it, relief and dread twining together. The room, once heavy with silence, surged into motion — other Wrens lifting their heads, pens scratching, voices low with quick translation. After hours of empty static, the violence of sound was almost unbearable, but Nancy clung to it, forcing her hand steady. For better or worse, the world had spoken again.

Each burst of German chatter made her heart lurch — *Rudel, torpedoes fired, one burning*. She scribbled frantically, her hand shaking, desperate to decode, to understand. She wanted to fling off the headphones and scream at the world to tell her, to stop hiding behind numbers and call signs. Instead, she swallowed hard and kept writing, her letters crooked, smudged with sweat.

German intercepts broke with Allied intercepts — *Sword, Omaha, Juno…*

When the duty officer finally came round with the morning reports, her breath snagged in her throat. The words blurred as she read: Tanker lost. Escort engaged. Survivors uncertain. No ship names, no confirmation, just another cold, incomplete tally. Nancy pressed her fist to her lips, forcing the sob down. The others carried on, business as usual, but she could barely sit still. Every nerve in her body screamed for news, any news. Until she knew, she would go on listening, frantic, her whole world narrowed to the hiss of static and the dread of silence.

The clock above the signals board ticked past the end of her shift, but Nancy stayed rooted to her chair, headphones pressed so tightly they bruised her ears. Her pencil hovered, ready, though the lines on her pad had long since blurred into nonsense.

A hand touched her shoulder. "That's enough, Carter," Elsie said, her voice firm but not unkind. "You've been on duty since dawn. Go back to the dorm, get some rest."

Nancy shook her head, not daring to lift her eyes from the dials. "I can't. Not yet."

Elsie carried herself with the calm authority of a woman who had seen enough of life to be neither easily rattled nor easily deceived. Her face was softened by kindness, her eyes quick to catch the struggles of the younger girls under her watch, yet there was a quiet strength in her posture that brooked no nonsense. She spoke gently, rarely raising her voice, but her words carried weight all the same — fairness and firmness woven together. To the Wrens, she was both guide and guardian, offering encouragement when nerves frayed, but never hesitating to set them straight when duty demanded it. There was a steadiness in her presence, a reassuring strength that reminded them all that women could lead with grace as well as grit.

Elsie crouched beside her, lowering her voice so the others wouldn't hear. "Listen to me. You'll be no use half-dead at your desk. Whatever happens out there, it won't change whether you sit here or lie in a bunk for three hours' sleep."

Nancy swallowed, her throat raw. "But… what if there's a signal, what if I miss—"

Elsie's gaze softened, the lines in her face deeper than usual. "If there's news, it'll keep. That's the cruel thing about this job — the world can end in a heartbeat, and still we're told to wait. You can't make the sea move faster by staring at it."

Nancy clenched her fists in her lap, fighting the sting in her eyes. She wanted to argue, to beg to stay, but the weight in her chest was too heavy. Slowly, reluctantly, she pulled the headphones down and set them on the desk.

"I'll only rest if they tell us something soon," she whispered.

Elsie squeezed her arm, understanding without saying so. "Then pray for quiet, Nance. Sometimes no news really is the best we'll get."

Nancy nodded faintly, but as she left the hut, the static still rang in her ears, merciless, filling the silence where Fred's name should have been.

Dawn was almost drawing as Nancy made her way back to her bunk. Unable to eat, Nancy had contemplated that it may be better to sleep it off. Fighting with tireless thoughts keeping her from falling into a deep sleep, eventually it took her.

Nancy tossed beneath her blanket, her body twisting as though to escape some unseen grip. In her dream the static roared, a harsh, endless hiss that filled her head until it was all she could hear. She pressed the headphones tighter, desperate to catch a voice, a word, anything — but the silence that followed was worse, vast and suffocating. Faces blurred through the fog of her sleep: sailors slipping beneath black water, Edward's name carved in stone, Fred vanishing into the grey mist of the sea. She called out but no sound left her lips, only the shriek of the wireless, loud and merciless. Her hands clenched the sheets as though they were logbooks, her breath shallow, her heart beating in a rhythm of fear. Even in slumber, the war would not let her rest.

Nancy, completely exhausted and restless, woke through broken sleep. Each time the same thought:

There is no peace in war.

ONLY A LETTER AWAY

Nancy and Mary pushed open the heavy door of the barracks, the familiar hum of voices and shuffle of boots rising to meet them. At once, they saw the small crowd gathered around the duty desk, Wrens craning their necks with that unmistakable air of anticipation. The post had come. A handful of envelopes lay waiting, their corners smudged from travel, the inked names leaping out like treasures from another world.

Mary nudged Nancy gently with her elbow, eyes alight. "Go on, check—maybe today's your lucky day." Sure enough, when Nancy's name was called, a neat white envelope was pressed into her hand, her heart lifting at the familiar scrawl of Fred's writing across the front. For a moment, she held it close, feeling the weight of it, the distance it had crossed to reach her. Around them, the barracks buzzed with the rustle of paper and laughter, a brief burst of warmth and connection in the middle of the war.

As the envelope touched her hand, Nancy felt an immense relief flood through her body, so sudden it nearly stole her breath. Her throat tightened, her eyes pricking as though tears might come before she could stop them. For days she had told herself not to hope too much, not to expect a letter, and yet the sight of Fred's familiar handwriting dissolved all that careful restraint in an instant. The distance between them seemed to shrink, just for that moment, to the space between the ink and the paper in her hands. She pressed the letter close against her chest, reassuring herself, afraid that if she loosened her grip it might vanish like a dream.

My Dearest Nancy,

It does me more good than you could know to sit down with pen and paper and write to you. Out here, the days run together, and sometimes I think I'd forget who I am if not for the thought of you waiting at home.

We've come through a hard spell. The sea itself is cruel enough, but these last weeks have been worse still. We've taken damage, and though Fury carries on, she is not the ship she was. We lost good men, Nancy. Too many. I find it hard to look their mates in the eye, knowing I was spared when others weren't. Survivor's guilt, they call it, but words don't make it easier. I carry their faces with me, every hour, and I wonder why I am still here when they are not.

As though the enemy were not punishment enough, the weather turned against us too. A storm came down like the wrath of God himself—black skies, waves higher than the deck, timbers groaning as though the ship would split. Fury bore it, but not without scars. Storm damage keeps us busy from dawn till dusk, patching and hammering to make her seaworthy again. She's a proud ship, but she has been battered.

Still, I write to you, and that is enough to keep me steady. I think of your face when the wind howls through the rigging, I think of your hands when mine are numb from cold, and I think of your voice when the world is all noise and chaos. It's you, Nancy, who gives me the strength to endure.

Until I can see you again, know that every word I write is a step closer to home.

Yours always,

Fred

Nancy's hands trembled as she folded the letter closed, pressing it tightly between her palms as if she could anchor Fred to her through the paper alone. Relief poured through her in waves so strong she almost felt weak beneath it, her chest loosening after days of being wound tight as wire. For the first time since that dreadful silence on the line, she could breathe again—truly breathe—and the heaviness that had sat on her heart for over a week finally eased.

Mary, perched quietly on the edge of the bunk, she watched her friend with soft eyes. She had seen Nancy's strain, the way she had carried on each day as though nothing was wrong, while her shoulders told a different story. Now, as Nancy drew a shaky breath and let it out, Mary thought it was as though she was watching life return to her. "There you are," she whispered to herself, almost too softly for Nancy to hear.

The fragile calm was short-lived. Across the room, a quiet sob broke the hush, sharp enough to turn heads. Francis sat on her bunk, a thin blue envelope crumpled in her hands. Her face was pale, eyes fixed on the page as though rereading it might conjure a different truth.

"No news," she choked, voice breaking. "Weeks gone by, and still nothing. They don't know where he is."

At once the mood shifted. Mary slipped from Nancy's side and was already at Francis's shoulder, an arm wrapping gently around her. Elsie crossed the room with a clean handkerchief, pressing it into Francis's hand. One by one the girls drew nearer, their chatter falling away into murmurs of comfort.

Nancy folded Fred's letter carefully, guilt and gratitude twisting inside her chest, and joined them. She laid a hand over Francis's, gentle and warm. "You're not alone," she said softly, and the circle of Wrens tightened, their small strength shared between them. Relief and grief, hope and fear—they all lived side by side in the barracks, stitched together by the bond of women waiting.

Francis bent her head, shoulders trembling, and for a moment it seemed as though the weight of silence might crush her. Mary gave her a gentle squeeze, speaking in the calm, level voice she always used when nerves ran high. "It doesn't mean the worst, love. No news is just that—no news. You know how the post is, letters get lost, or ships get diverted."

Elsie sat herself down firmly on the other side, slipping an arm round Francis's waist as though sheer stubbornness could hold her together. "My cousin didn't hear a word for two months, and then three letters turned up at once," she said with conviction. "Bet you he's cursing the Navy postmaster same as the rest of us."

A ripple of agreement came from the other bunks. Someone chimed in about their brother whose letters had crossed the ocean twice before they found him, another told of parcels arriving months out of date, chocolate melted and re-set into odd shapes.

Francis gave a broken laugh through her tears, the faintest smile tugging at the corner of her mouth. She dabbed at her eyes with Elsie's handkerchief, the colour slowly returning to her cheeks. Nancy reached across, taking her free hand in both of her own.

"Hold on to that," she said softly. "The waiting's the hardest, but we'll face it together. Every one of us."

The girls pressed in close, their warmth surrounding her, until Francis let out a long, shuddering breath and nodded. The sorrow wasn't gone, but it was eased—carried now by many shoulders, not hers alone.

Elsie broke the heavy mood first, nudging Francis with a sly grin. "Cheer up, love. You'll have half the dockyard queueing for a dance with you again, at the next dance. Bet you five Woodbines the first sailor who asks is taller than the clock tower."

That earned a round of laughter, and Mary jumped in quickly. "Aye, but I warn you—watch the ones who drink too quick. All charm till the rum catches them, then you'll be carrying them back to barracks."

Nancy shook her head, unable to stop her smile. "And here I thought sailors were meant to be strong."

"Oh, they are," Elsie said with mock solemnity, "just not strong enough to hold their liquor."

The bunks erupted with knowing chuckles, each girl tossing in a story—of a lad who tried to serenade the wrong girl after one tot too many, of another who'd fallen asleep mid-dance with his head on her shoulder. Even Francis managed a proper laugh, her eyes still damp but her face lighter.

By the time lights-out came, the barracks hummed with whispered jokes and sly giggles, the shadows filled with the sound of girls teasing and gossiping. The grief hadn't vanished, but it was dulled, tucked away beneath the warm, defiant laughter that only young women at war could muster.

⚓

All around was hushed except for the steady clatter of the typewriter and the faint crackle of the wireless. Nancy sat with her headphones pressed tight, the pencil flying across her pad as she caught fragments from the ether—numbers, letters, short clipped words carried over the static. Beside her, Mary straightened suddenly, brow furrowed.

"Did you hear that?" Mary whispered, pulling one earpiece away as though to be sure. "Sword… Juno… they keep repeating."

Nancy paused, the scratch of her pencil stilled. A ripple of recognition ran through her, quick and cold. She had heard those words before—not just once, but again and again, woven through transmissions in the past week. "Yes," she said quietly, eyes narrowing. "I've caught them too."

Mary frowned, glancing toward the duty officer's closed door. "They don't sound like the usual codes, and it's not just British—it's American voices too. What does it mean?"

Nancy shook her head, her voice certain though her stomach fluttered uneasily. "I don't know, but it means something. They wouldn't keep using the same words if it didn't." She looked back to her pad, the names stark on the page: *Sword. Juno. Gold.* Familiar now, and yet mysterious. She tried to swallow the uneasy knot forming in her throat.

Mary lowered her voice further, her eyes bright with curiosity. "Do you think we're supposed to hear it?"

Nancy didn't answer. Instead, she slid her pencil behind her ear and stared down at the words she'd written. She had no explanation, no answers—

only the gnawing certainty that something was moving beneath the surface, gathering like a storm on the horizon.

BOMBS OVER BASE

The sirens had barely begun their wail when the first wave came in low over the Flow. Nancy burst from the barracks with the others, the night sky alive with the thrum of engines. Searchlights stabbed upward, their beams catching the gleam of black-crossed wings.

"Stukas!" someone cried.

The shriek of bombs followed. Nancy flinched as the ground convulsed, the shockwave slamming her chest. She stumbled, ears ringing, the sky torn with fire.

Out on the water, a tanker lay moored against the pier — her vast hull black against the harbour lights, crammed with precious fuel for the fleet. Nancy's stomach clenched. Too big. Too slow. Too vulnerable.

The next stick of bombs found her.

The explosion ripped through the night, a thunderclap that split the harbour wide open. Flames shot skyward, a tower of fire and smoke, lighting the Flow as though dawn had come too early. The tanker's steel plates buckled like paper, hurling debris into the air. Men on deck were flung into the water, their screams cutting through the roar.

Nancy's breath caught. She had no training for this, no orders other than to take cover, but her legs carried her forward anyway, towards the shoreline where ratings and Wrens were already converging. The heat seared her face even from a hundred yards away.

"Keep back!" an officer shouted, arms spread wide. "Fuel's going up!"

Men were thrashing in the water, dark shapes against the burning reflection. Oil spread across the surface, igniting where it touched the flames, trapping the survivors in a ring of fire.

Nancy saw one man clawing toward the shore, arms flailing weakly before he slipped beneath. Another surfaced, coughing, his uniform alight. A launch swung out to reach them, sailors dousing themselves with seawater as they dragged their comrades aboard.

The tanker groaned, her bow dipping, smoke pouring from ruptured tanks. Another explosion thundered, sending a geyser of fire shooting skyward. The blast knocked Nancy flat, the heat baking her skin. She tasted grit and smoke, choking.

Hands hauled her up — Mary, her face pale, shouting something, Nancy couldn't hear through the ringing in her ears. All she could see was the burning ship, the water around her slick with death.

Precious fuel lost. Precious lives lost. The Flow itself aflame.

Still the bombers came, their engines snarling overhead, Luftwaffe searching for more to destroy.

The siren shrieked like a living thing, splitting the stillness of the Scottish night. Nancy jolted upright from her bunk, the wool blanket tangling at her legs. For one disoriented heartbeat she thought she was still in her dream… nightmare, or it was another drill. Then the earth shuddered with the low boom of distant guns, and she knew this was no exercise.

Nancy startled, her eyes drawn instinctively to the door. Was it the Luftwaffe? The thought coiled in her stomach, unbidden but sharp. She pictured the German war machines rising from their hidden airfields, engines screaming, wings glinting as they cut across the clouds. Even in quiet moments, she could never quite silence the dread that at any second the horizon might darken with them, the whistle of bombs chasing her from thought.

Nancy felt the vibration first—a low, unsettling thrum that seemed to come from beneath the earth itself. She froze, the hair on her arms prickling, just as the first faint drone of engines rolled in from the distance. It was a sound everyone on the base knew too well: the Luftwaffe coming in across the water.

"Air raid! Move!" a woman's voice shouted. Boots thundered across the dormitory floor.

Nancy snatched her greatcoat and gas mask from the peg, her hands fumbling as she tried to fasten the buttons. Adrenaline rushing through her body. The room filled with Wrens pulling on uniforms in the dark, shoving feet into shoes, the sharp tang of fear thick in the air.

Outside, the night sky glowed faintly orange to the east. Searchlights clawed upward, beams cutting through low cloud. The drone of engines — dozens of them — rolled over the base like an oncoming storm.

Searchlights snapped to life, slicing the night sky with cold beams. The engines grew louder, filling the air with a relentless, mechanical roar. Then came the first whistle—shrill, cutting—and the earth split open with a shuddering explosion that sent dust and grit rattling against the huts. The ground lurched beneath Nancy's feet, throwing her to one knee, her ears ringing. Glass exploded somewhere nearby, screams breaking out as figures rushed for the shelters. The acrid smell of smoke and cordite spread quickly, mixing with the salt tang of the sea. Overhead, the black silhouettes of planes wheeled and dived like predators circling prey.

Nancy ran with the others toward the shelter trench, the ground uneven beneath her. A whistle shrieked overhead, followed by the earth-rattling crash of a bomb. The ground heaved, throwing her sideways into Mary. They clung to each other, coughing through dust and grit.

Around them Nancy noticed Jack picking up Phyllis, another Wren, who had tumbled in the chaos. Elsie was shuffling people into the bunker, pointing and commanding, as Talbot was scuffling to encourage Elsie to get inside to safety.

"Keep running!" Mary shouted, though her voice was nearly swallowed by the chaos.

Explosions burst closer now — one, then another, shaking windows, rattling the wireless hut at the edge of the yard. Nancy's heart clenched. *The wireless logs… the signals room… if that goes, half the fleet is blind.*

Another whistle — nearer this time. Instinct yanked Nancy to the ground. The bomb struck with a deafening roar only a hundred yards or so away. Heat washed over her, and she felt grit sting her face. When she scrambled up, ears ringing, she saw the wireless hut blazing.

"Nancy!" Mary tugged her arm, trying to drag her toward the trench.

Nancy's gaze locked on the flames. Inside the hut were the records — convoy schedules, codes, everything the Navy needed to keep its ships alive. If the fire spread, if those papers burned…

She hesitated, torn between survival and duty. Smoke billowed into the night, acrid and choking. Around her, Wrens and ratings scrambled for cover. Somewhere, anti-aircraft guns hammered, tracers stabbing at the enemy planes.

Nancy made her choice. She pulled free of Mary's grasp and sprinted toward the hut.

Behind her, she could hear the faint cry of Mary "Now isn't the time to try and be a hero."

The heat was unbearable before Nancy even entered the wireless hut. Sparks whipped through the night air, stinging her skin. She pulled her greatcoat over her mouth and nose and forced herself forward, boots crunching on the smashed glass, scattered all around.

The door hung from its hinges, the frame blackened. Inside, the room was thick with smoke, the wireless set sparking like a wounded beast. Flames licked up the walls, devouring paper as they climbed.

Nancy's eyes stung, but she could still see the log cabinet against the far wall. The convoy records. The only copies until they were sent out.

She shoved forward, coughing violently as the smoke clawed down her throat. Her hands trembled as she yanked open the cabinet drawer. Logs tumbled out, pages already curling at the edges from the heat. She seized as many as she could, clutching them to her chest.

Another explosion rocked the base, showering her with plaster. The ceiling groaned. For a moment, panic nearly rooted her to the spot. What if the roof collapses? What if this is the last thing I ever do?

For the briefest of seconds, she thought of Edward — the first man she had loved, gone too soon, buried beneath the steel and explosions in the Atlantic. Followed by a thought of Fred — alive somewhere out there, relying on the very words she held in her arms.

Her legs moved. She staggered back through the choking haze toward the doorway.

Just as she reached it, a figure loomed in the smoke. A man —, one of the petty officers, she thought, though she couldn't make out his face. He froze when he saw the bundle in her arms.

"You shouldn't be in here!" he barked, voice rough. "Drop those — get out!"

Nancy blinked, disoriented. Why would he tell her to drop the logs? Every instinct screamed to protect them.

"I'm saving them!" she shot back, forcing her way past the smoke wrapped figure. His hand twitched, as though he meant to snatch them, but another beam of fire burst overhead, and he stumbled back instead.

She didn't stop to question it. She ran, out into the night air, collapsing just short of the trench with the logs still pressed tight to her chest.

Hands dragged her down into cover. Mary's face swam into view, pale with fear, and speckled with soot.

Pressed shoulder to shoulder in the air-raid shelter, Nancy could hear the frightened breaths of the women around her, quick and shallow, punctuated by whispered prayers. Mary's hand found hers in the dark, squeezing hard enough to hurt, grounding her. The ceiling above them rattled with each detonation, dust filtering down in thin streams that caught in the lamplight. Nancy clenched her jaw, forcing herself not to imagine the bombs falling closer, the huts above them burning, or the ships in harbour struck and sinking. She told herself that fear was wasted energy—but her heart still hammered, each beat louder than the previous.

"You mad fool!" Mary gasped, breathlessly, gripping her shoulders. "You could have been killed!"

Nancy coughed hard, her lungs raw, but managed to rasp: "Better me than the convoys."

Mary tried to scold her again, but the words stuck in her throat. She only squeezed Nancy's hand — tight, fierce — as bombs thundered overhead.

Nancy looked down at her tattered stockings and bloodied knee. "Guess I will have to get the gravy browning out so it looks like I am wearing seams." Nancy whispered to Mary, her sense of humour subtly shining through in the most desperate of times.

Nancy's attention quickly turned to the charred, singed pages in her arms. They smelled of smoke and survival. Something else nagged at her, sharp and unsettling.

The figure in the smoke. His hesitation. His words.

Why had he wanted her to drop them?

⚓

When at last the drone of engines faded, the silence that settled was more suffocating than the chaos before. They emerged to a world shrouded in smoke, the air thick with the metallic tang of blood and the acrid stench of fire. Buildings smouldered, their outlines jagged and unfamiliar, while wardens shouted orders above the crackle of flames. Nancy stared at the devastation—the collapsed roof of the signals hut, the crater gouged deep into the parade ground, the stretcher-bearers hurrying past with distressed emotion displayed on their faces. The base was the same, yet entirely altered, as though some fragile layer of normality had been stripped away in a single night.

By dawn, the smoke had thinned into a grey haze that clung low over the harbour. The fires were out, though the choking stench of burned fuel still hung heavy in the air. The tanker lay half-submerged, her twisted hulk listing against the pier, gulls already circling overhead as if the sea itself had claimed her.

Nancy picked her way across the yard, boots grating across the splintered glass and scattered brick. Wrens and sailors moved in weary silence, clearing debris, patching holes, rolling new cables across the charred ground. The wireless hut was gone, reduced to a blackened frame, but already a fresh set had been rigged in a drafty storeroom nearby. New equipment arrived on the back of lorries, the crates stencilled with bold white letters — proof that the work would not stop, no matter the cost.

Exhaustion tugged at Nancy's limbs, but her pencil was sharp, her logbook ready. Every signal she copied that morning felt like defiance: numbers against the silence, a thin line holding chaos at bay.

Around her, men hauled wreckage, women swept broken tiles into piles, officers barked orders to rebuild. The base bore its scars openly, but it was alive.

Mary brushed past with a broom, her hair still dusted with soot. "You'd never know we'd been bombed flat a few hours ago," she said with a weak smile.

Nancy managed a nod, though her throat was tight. She knew the truth: the dead couldn't be swept away with the rubble. Yet as the sun broke through the haze, casting a pale gold over the battered yard outside, she felt a flicker of resolve kindle in her chest. The bombs had come and gone, but they were still here. Still listening. Still fighting.

Nancy could still see him — the man's outline blurred in smoke, the way his hand had twitched as though reaching for the bundle of papers, the sharp bark of his voice: *Drop those. Get out.*

It replayed in Nancy's mind with every scratch of her pencil. Why tell her to leave the logs behind? Why hesitate, as if the codes were more dangerous than the flames themselves?

It wasn't the first oddity, either. The ink blotted code sheet. The slip of paper missing from her logbook, only to reappear two days later in the wrong order. A decoded message filed in the wrong folder, though she was certain she hadn't touched it. Small things, so easy to dismiss as coincidence — yet together they pricked at her nerves like splinters.

She told herself she was tired, seeing patterns where none existed. The thought lingered: what if someone wanted her to doubt herself? Or worse — what if someone wanted the convoys blind, and she had stumbled into their way?

Nancy bent back over the wireless, forcing her hand steady. Still, in the back of her mind, the question refused to leave.

Who was he? And what game was being played in the shadows of this base?

SURVIVAL OF FAITH

Fred leaned against the cold steel bulkhead, the ship rolling gently beneath his boots. The sea was calm for once, but his nerves weren't. He had just finished his watch when the signal officer found him, a folded dispatch clutched in one hand.

"Message from the base, sir," the young officer said. "Thought you'd want to see it."

Fred frowned and took the paper. It wasn't often anything personal came through official channels. He unfolded it, eyes scanning quickly.

At first, the words barely registered. Then they slammed into him.

```
Air raid over coastal base...
extensive damage... wireless hut destroyed...
records saved by quick action of WRNS
telegraphist Nancy Carter...
```

Fred froze, the letters swimming. Nancy.

He read the line again, hardly breathing. She had run *into* a burning building to save signals — to save *his* fleet. Her name, printed in stiff naval type, leapt off the page like a beacon.

For a moment, pride surged through him, so fierce it almost buckled his knees. He could picture her, stubborn, chin lifted in defiance, refusing to yield even to fire. God, she was braver than half the men he served with.

Pride and admiration were soon replaced by feelings much colder, sharper. Dread crept into Fred's mind: *What if she'd been killed?*

The dispatch hadn't said she was unharmed. Just that she had acted. Fred's mind betrayed him, painting the image too vividly — Nancy's hair caught with sparks, her lungs filling with smoke, her body lying under rubble as others carried her out too late.

He pressed the paper to his chest, closing his eyes. Edward's face flashed in his memory — Edward, the golden boy lost too soon, the one Nancy had loved first. Fred thought, with a sick twist in his gut: *She deserves better than waiting for another coffin.*

When he opened his eyes again, the deck was noisy with laughter and clinking mugs, but Fred felt apart from it, weighed down by something heavy. Survivor's guilt. Pride. Fear. Love, tangled with all of it.

He folded the dispatch carefully, sliding it inside his jacket. Close to his heart, where he carried Nancy's letters.

Under his breath, he murmured, "Hold on, Nance. I need you to keep breathing, I will come home to you. To keep you safe."

Fred assumed his position, back leaned against the cold grey metal, staring out to the endless horizon, he caught himself picturing the tea shop — Nancy's eyes downcast, her smile flickering when she teased him. It was a fragile little flame of memory, but it burned against the Atlantic like a lantern.

⚓

The base still smelled of smoke days later, a bitter tang that clung to hair and uniforms no matter how much they scrubbed. Nancy sat in the wireless hut's temporary replacement — a draughty storeroom hastily filled with equipment. She bent over her set, tuning carefully, pencil poised over her log sheet.

Nancy shifted on the hard bench, reaching down to scratch an itch where her skirt rubbed uncomfortably against her leg. When her fingers came away, she noticed the faint smudge of brown on her hand, the tell-tale stain of the gravy browning she had rubbed carefully onto her calves that morning to mimic stockings. It had become part of her routine now, ever since the last air raid had left the shops bare and the few pairs she owned snagged beyond repair. She rubbed her thumb across the mark, half-smiling at the absurdity of it all—this makeshift trick of vanity, clinging to the small rituals of normal life in a world that had stripped so much away.

Nancy wiped the smear absently against her skirt and let her hand rest there a moment longer. She thought of the other women she passed each day—on the base, and in the village. They all made the same little compromises: gravy browning for stockings, coats patched and repatched until the fabric grew thin. Small acts, almost invisible, yet they spoke of something larger—an insistence on holding on to normality, to dignity, in a world determined to wear them down. It wasn't vanity so much as defiance, Nancy realised. A refusal to let the war strip everything away.

She tried to focus, but the whispers kept cutting through the static.

"Reckless, running in like that. Could've lost the whole hut." One of the voices muttered.

"Or maybe she knew what she was looking for…"

Nancy's hand trembled on the dial. She didn't have to turn to know who was speaking. Wren, Iris Moffatt — sharp-tongued, ambitious, always watching her. Nancy had never understood why Iris disliked her, but lately, her barbed comments had grown bolder.

"She was the only one inside, wasn't she?" Iris said, her voice carrying just enough to be overheard. "Funny how the logs were saved, but half the signals set went up in flames. Almost like someone chose what to rescue."

Nancy's stomach dropped. She forced herself to keep writing, to ignore it, but heat prickled the back of her neck. Around her, a few girls exchanged uneasy glances, not daring to intervene.

When her shift ended, Nancy stepped into the cold evening air, her head spinning. She had done her duty — nothing more, nothing less. Now, thanks to Iris, her actions were being twisted into something suspect.

Nancy caught herself thinking of Iris Moffatt again, her sharp tongue and watchful eyes. There was something in the woman's manner that set her on edge — the way her smile never reached her eyes, the way she always seemed to be listening rather than speaking. Why did she dislike her so much? Was it because Iris had been so quick to step onto the dance floor with Fred, all those months ago, her laughter too loud, her hand lingering too long? Or was it the contrast with Elsie — who, for all her fairness and kindness, always seemed to go out of her way to shield Nancy, to treat her with a softness she didn't always extend to others? Nancy tried to shake it off, telling herself it was foolish jealousy, or nerves, made worse by long watches and too little sleep. Still, the feeling lingered — that Iris Moffatt was not what she pretended to be.

As she crossed the yard, Commander Talbot intercepted her. His expression was unreadable, hands clasped behind his back.

"Carter," he said curtly. "A word."

Her breath caught. This was it — the doubts, the suspicion, the way her logs had already been questioned once. Her chest tightened.

"Yes, sir?"

Talbot studied her, eyes narrowing slightly. "You've been commended for quick thinking. But some of your colleagues are… less convinced. I don't need to remind you, trust is everything in this work. One misstep, and men die."

Nancy swallowed hard. "I understand, sir."

He nodded, then leaned closer. "See that you do."

When he walked away, Nancy stood frozen, pulse racing. It wasn't fair. She'd risked her life for those papers. And yet — here she was, feeling under suspicion.

That night, when she sat down to write to Fred, her hand hesitated over the page. She wanted to pour everything out — the whispers, the doubt, the loneliness. What good would it do? He had enough burdens at sea without hers weighing him down.

So she tore the page in half and began again.

My Dearest Fred,

I hope this finds you safe. I heard your convoy made it through. I've been thinking of you every night, and I wonder if you think of me, too…

Her duty demanded silence. Her heart demanded honesty. For the first time, Nancy felt the strain of being pulled in two directions at once.

Nancy sat on the edge of her bunk, unpinning her hair with slow, heavy hands. The day's static still rang in her ears, a hiss she couldn't shake. Mary dropped onto the bed beside her, arms folded, face set in a way Nancy didn't like.

"You've heard it, haven't you?" Mary said quietly.

Nancy frowned. "Heard what?"

"The whispers. About a spy. In Signals."

Nancy's stomach tightened. She forced a shrug. "There are always rumours. People have nothing better to do when they're tired."

Mary shook her head, jaw tight. "It's more than that, Nance. Iris Moffatt's been saying things. That you were the last in the hut before the fire. That you've made mistakes in the logs. That you always seem to know more than you should."

Nancy snapped her head round, eyes flashing. "That's ridiculous. You know me better than that, Mary."

"I do." Mary's voice softened, but the worry stayed. "… others don't, and they're listening to her. You've been under suspicion before — Talbot nearly said as much."

Nancy pressed her fists against her knees, fighting the hot surge of anger and fear. "So what? You think I should run to him and beg him to believe me?"

Mary leaned closer, gripping her hand. "I think you should speak to him before she twists things further. Or Elsie — she'd listen. You can't let it fester, Nance. Once a rumour starts…" She shook her head in the pause. "It doesn't stop."

Nancy swallowed hard, her throat aching. Mary's hand was warm, but the words stung all the same. Her best friend was warning her — and warning meant doubt.

"Maybe I should," Nancy whispered at last, though the thought of baring herself to Talbot's cool gaze made her stomach churn. "God help me, Mary — I'm telling the truth."

"I know." Mary squeezed her hand tighter, though her eyes still held shadows. "I just don't want to lose you to whispers before the war ever gets the chance."

⚓

The base carried a tautness that hadn't been there before. Conversations hushed as people passed in corridors, and the air itself seemed to bristle with watchfulness. Even the ordinary rhythms—boots on the parade ground, the typewriters rattling in the signals hut, the coded bursts of Morse—felt somehow sharpened, as though everyone was waiting for something unseen to break. Nancy noticed the glances exchanged between colleagues, the way voices dropped when footsteps approached. Secrets hung in the air like smoke.

Nancy woke to the clatter of boots in the corridor and the murmur of voices pitched low with unease. For a moment she thought she'd overslept, that her shift had already begun, but when she sat up the dormitory was still dim with early light. Mary was already fastening her tunic, her face drawn.

"What's happened?" Nancy asked, pushing back the blanket.

"Signals room," Mary muttered. "Fuse blew in the night. Half the set's dead, and one of the cables —" she hesitated, glancing at the other Wrens still dressing, "— looks like it's been cut."

Nancy's stomach dropped. "Cut?"

Mary gave a shrug that wasn't convincing. "That's what they're saying. It could've been clumsiness, someone tripping in the dark. But after—" She left the thought unfinished.

By the time Nancy reached the storeroom that had been converted into their new hut, the place was a jumble of activity. Elsie stood with her hands on her hips, sharp-eyed as sailors dragged in spare equipment. The air smelled of hot metal and singed wiring.

"Keep moving, girls," Elsie snapped. "We'll be back on the air before breakfast."

Nancy took her place at a desk, but her hands wouldn't stop trembling. A fuse blowing was nothing unusual — the kit was temperamental at the best of times — but a cleanly severed cable? That wasn't chance.

Her gaze flicked across the room. Iris Moffatt stood with two other Wrens near the door, whispering. When she caught Nancy looking, her smile curved — thin, knowing, like a cat watching a cornered mouse. Nancy noticed, Lieutenant Harvey stood leaning against the door frame, lingering, watching the commotion, not helping drive the critical activities going on about the place.

Nancy bent over her pad, forcing her pencil steady, but the unease gnawed deeper. First the fire, then the whispers, now this. The accidents were adding up, and she knew in her bones they weren't accidents at all.

⚓

In hopes of distraction, Mary insisted Nancy and her go for a walk and get some fresh air after their shift in the signals. The harbour was never truly quiet. Even at dawn, gulls wheeled overhead in ragged formation, their cries sharp against the roll of the tide. Fishing boats rocked against their moorings, their timbers creaking like old bones, and the scent of tar and salt carried on the wind. Beyond the breakwater, the open sea stretched in a restless expanse of pewter grey, a reminder that somewhere out there men fought battles unseen. Along the cobbled quayside, women in shawls moved briskly with baskets, their footsteps echoing as they passed the Wrens in their neat uniforms. The war had changed the rhythm of the place—once a sleepy outpost, now every arrival or departure of a ship drew eyes to the horizon, hope and dread bound together.

Nancy adjusted the collar of her greatcoat against the sting of the wind, her boots clicking on the stone. Beside her, Mary linked arms, laughing at something only half a joke, about Nancy's drawn-on stockings her breath puffing out in a white cloud. They were part of the tide themselves now, as much a feature of the base as the signal masts bristling above the rooftops. Everywhere Nancy looked there were signs of duty—men in navy blues striding towards the docks, dockyard workers with hands blackened from coal dust, messages carried swiftly in dispatch bags. Yet between all of it lingered an air of ordinary life: the smell of fresh bread from the bakery on the corner, the chatter of children chasing each other by the steps, a dog barking at the commotion of a ship preparing to cast off.

Nancy found her gaze drawn, as always, to the ships that lay moored and ready. Their hulls loomed dark and formidable, names stencilled in crisp white letters, each one a reminder that Fred might have been aboard something not unlike them. She couldn't help but imagine him at that moment—on deck somewhere across the ocean, salt spray cutting at his face, the constant rumble of engines beneath his feet. It was foolish, she told herself, to think she could sense his presence in the wind or the waves. Yet, she did. Each roll of the tide, each signal flag raised, seemed to carry some whisper of him back to her.

The war was everywhere in small, intrusive ways. Posters on the brick walls urged them to "Keep Mum, She's Not So Dumb" or "Careless Talk Costs Lives." Windows were criss-crossed with tape against air raids. The faint drumming of typewriters spilled from an office window, punctuated by the clatter of bicycles on cobbles as messengers hurried past. Even the church bells had a different sound now—less of a Sunday summons, more of a call to keep faith alive in a world threatened by shadows. Still, the sea went on rolling, as if indifferent to the comings and goings of men and their wars.

SUSPICION ARISES

Nancy paused in the doorway of the barracks, her eyes falling on Mary bent over the small desk by her bunk. The lamplight caught the curve of her cheek, the tip of her tongue peeking at the corner of her mouth as she carefully penned her words. Two envelopes lay ready at her elbow—one already addressed to her brother, the other blank, waiting.

Curious, Nancy stepped closer, and Mary gave a little start before slipping her hand over the second envelope. A faint colour rose in her cheeks.

"Another letter home?" Nancy asked gently.

Mary nodded, then hesitated, her gaze dropping to the half-finished page before her. “One for my brother, yes. And… another.” She tapped the second envelope with her fingertip, not quite meeting Nancy’s eyes. “For a lad I met at the dance. A sailor. We’ve been writing, just here and there.”

Nancy blinked in surprise, a smile tugging faintly at her lips. She realised, suddenly, how much she had missed in her own world, so utterly consumed by thoughts of Fred that she hadn’t noticed Mary quietly carrying her own little secret.

Mary gave a soft shrug, almost apologetic. “It’s nothing to boast about. War isn’t the time for romance, not really. I didn’t want to make it sound bigger than it is. But—” she trailed off, a wistful warmth in her eyes, “it’s nice to have someone write your name. To remind you you’re more than just a uniform.”

Nancy’s heart squeezed at that, the ache of longing for Fred mingling with affection for her friend. She reached to touch Mary’s shoulder, offering a smile. “I think that’s something worth holding on to.”

Mary gave a small laugh, though it wavered. "He's not Fred, of course. Not the sort of love that anchors you." She folded the page neatly, slipping it into the envelope with care. "But it's something. A spark, I suppose. Something to remind me the world isn't only duty and loss."

Nancy watched her seal the letter, feeling both touched and chastened. She had been so swept up in her own longing for Fred that she had missed this gentle thread of hope unfolding right beside her. She reached across, giving Mary's hand a squeeze. "Then keep writing. Even the smallest sparks matter."

The two women shared a quiet smile, the lamplight catching the shadows beneath their eyes. Outside, the night was heavy with silence, but in the little barracks, with ink still drying on paper, there lingered a sense of something softer—of lives and hearts still finding a way to beat despite the war pressing in around them.

⚓

Nancy leafed through the logbook with her usual precision, eyes scanning the scrawled numbers and bearings from the night before. At first it was routine

— the endless chatter of the ether, call signs, coordinates. She stopped her pencil, thought casting a frown across her face.

One line was wrong. Not just sloppy, not just a mistyped digit. A bearing that, if followed, would have steered a convoy straight into the hunting grounds she knew the U-boats favoured. She traced it again with her finger, her chest tightening.

She turned the page. Another slip, hidden among the codes. Not enough to leap out at the untrained eye, but together… it was unmistakable. Someone had altered the logs. Someone had sent men to their deaths. The wolfpack took vessels with supplies and more importantly, lives, the log was not accurate.

Nancy's hands shook, her blood ran cold through her body, as she snapped the book closed.

Harvey shot a cold, sharp glance at Nancy as she stormed from the room.

She found Elsie in the storeroom-turned-hut, sleeves rolled up as she oversaw the replacement of a fuse box. "Ma'am, I need a word," Nancy said, her voice sharper than she meant.

Elsie glanced at her, one brow raised. "Make it quick."

Nancy thrust the log toward her. "Look here. These bearings don't match the intercepts we picked up. They were sent out as instructions—" She stopped, swallowing hard. "It put the convoy right in the path of a wolfpack."

Elsie took the book, flipping through with a practised eye. Her lips pressed tight. "Are you certain?"

"Yes, ma'am. I'm certain."

For a moment, the only sound was the scrape of sailors dragging cables across the floor. Then Elsie shut the log with a sharp snap.

"I'll see to it," she said curtly. "Leave this with me."

Nancy held-fast and didn't move. "With respect, ma'am, this isn't the first time. The fire, the cut cable — now this. It can't all be chance."

Elsie's eyes narrowed, cool as steel. "Careful, Carter. What you're suggesting is dangerous talk."

Nancy flushed but held her ground. "Not as dangerous as letting it happen again."

The silence between them stretched taut. Finally, Elsie nodded once, brisk. "Go back to your post, and keep this to yourself."

Nancy obeyed, but as she returned to her desk the unease in her stomach deepened. Elsie had listened, yes — but had she believed? If she had…, what would she do next?

The base had grown quieter since the raid, but not in a comforting way. It wasn't the hush of safety — it was the silence of watching eyes.

Nancy felt them on her constantly. The glances that lingered a little too long. Conversations that faltered when she entered a room. The way Iris always seemed to be near, listening, her lips curved in that thin smile that said she knew something Nancy didn't.

Even Mary, her closest friend, was becoming distant now. She still laughed with Nancy, still linked arms when they walked across the yard — but her laughter was too quick, too bright, and sometimes, when she thought Nancy wasn't looking, her eyes clouded with unease.

Nancy tried to tell herself it was all in her head. However, the evidence piled up like stones on her chest.

One evening, she returned to the dormitory to find her locker slightly ajar. The padlock hung loose, its shank twisted as if forced. Inside, her letters from Fred were scattered, envelopes torn open. Her pulse thundered as she gathered them up, heart aching at the violation.

Who had done it? And what were they looking for?

The next morning, Commander Talbot crossed her path, as she headed towards the hut for her shift. He didn't accuse her outright, but his tone cut sharper than before.

"Errors in the logs are mounting, Carter. This can't continue. Mis-direction, ink spills, missing codes. Either you're careless, or someone wants it to look that way. Neither is acceptable."

Nancy continued slowly with her stomach churning. The walls of the base felt narrower than ever, corridors closing in. Every footstep behind her seemed louder, every glance sharper, every whisper carrying her name.

Lying awake in the dark that night, Nancy tried to organise her thoughts. She could barely trust herself anymore.

What if they're right? What if I missed something, made a mistake that cost lives? What if Fred… what if Fred's next because of me?

The thought wrapped itself around her chest like barbed wire. She clutched Fred's last letter, crumpling the paper slightly in her grip. He had written about the stars — how he looked for them on quiet watches, imagining she was staring at the same sky.

She pressed the page to her lips, whispering into the dark: "I'm not a traitor, Fred. You have to believe me."

The night offered no answer, only the distant crash of waves against the harbour wall — and the gnawing certainty that someone was determined to see her fall.

Nancy had grown used to the constant pressure of the war, but lately it had changed shape, creeping closer. She caught herself studying faces in the hut—wondering, absurdly, who might not be what they seemed. It was a dangerous thought, one she scolded herself for entertaining. Yet, each time she passed Harvey in the passageway, she felt the prick of unease. There was something in the way his eyes flicked too quickly away, or how he always seemed to linger near a door as though listening for what was said inside. She told herself she was imagining it. Still, her instinct whispered otherwise.

HIS MAJESTYS NAVY

Nancy sat on the harbour wall, by the village clocktower, sunshine beating down, warm, but with chill air on the breeze when it fluttered through her hair. She sat, hand down beside her, palms flush on the top of the wall, fingers curled over in anticipation, as if she were trying to grip onto the wall, in excitement, frustration, anticipation…

Nancy looked out, across that crystal clear horizon, until she saw it. The smallest dark disruption in the horizon line. Then another, and another. The small dark blips became larger, she could count seven, eight, making out the shapes of ships. Seemingly so small all that distance away. As they crawled closer, they grew much larger, and with focus Nancy could count over sixteen vessels. She spotted the exact one she was patiently awaiting.

The destroyer, not the largest ship in the convoy, but certainly a large enough target. His destroyer. Fred's boat came into view. The butterflies set off in her stomach.

The destroyer's bow rose and fell against the waves, spray breaking white over her foredeck, the sunlight glinting off wet steel.

As she drew closer, the details came clear. Twin rows of anti-aircraft guns crouched along her decks, lean and angular, their barrels still trained skyward as though daring the enemy to return. The great forward turret, squat and heavy, loomed over the forecastle, while the aft gun sat ready under its shield, black with soot. Depth charge racks cluttered her stern, squat cylinders lashed tight and gleaming with salt.

The ship bore the scars of long weeks at sea. Rust streaked her plates, her paint dulled to a weary grey, patches darker where hurried repairs had been slapped on. She moved with the same predatory grace as ever, her screws thrumming a rhythmic beat through the water.

Even battered, she was a sight both proud and comforting: a blade of steel forged for the Atlantic war, bristling with guns yet carrying the hopes of every sailor aboard her. HMS *Fury*, home for a while — until the sea called her back again.

Her heart clenched. *Fury.*

More details leapt into view: signal flags snapping in the breeze, sailors lining the deck in dark silhouettes, their caps gleaming white. Nancy's pulse raced as her eyes darted from one figure to the next. So many faces, too far away to name. She knew she was foolish, that she couldn't possibly pick him out yet — still she searched, breath held, until her vision blurred.

Is he there? Did he make it?

The ship slid into the harbour, powerful yet battered, the water breaking away in smooth curls from her hull. To anyone else she was just another vessel, another destroyer back from convoy duty. To Nancy, she was everything — hope, fear, and the fragile thread of a future she scarcely dared to imagine.

The destroyer eased against the quay with a groan of ropes and the rattle of chains, her crew moving briskly to secure her. Shouts echoed across the water, mingling with the slap of waves against steel. Nancy stood rigid, every muscle taut, eyes scanning the line of sailors who moved to the gangway.

One by one they descended, boots striking the stone, shoulders hunched with fatigue. Some grinned, relieved to be ashore; others simply trudged past, too weary to notice the small knot of Wrens and villagers waiting to greet them. Nancy's breath caught with every face. Too tall. Too young. Not him.

Then she saw him.

Fred stepped onto the gangway, his cap tucked under one arm, his tunic smudged with salt and oil. He moved more slowly than the others, a faint stiffness in his stride, but when he reached the bottom and lifted his head, his eyes found hers across the crowd. Fred slipped free of the last knot of men, his stride uneven but determined.

The noise of the quay fell away. For a moment it was only the two of them, the distance between shrinking with every heartbeat. Nancy's throat tightened — she wanted to run to him, to throw her arms around him, to weep with relief. Propriety, discipline, the eyes of half the base — all held her still.

Fred stopped a pace before her, his voice low, hoarse with exhaustion. "Nance."

It was all he said, all he needed to say.

Nancy's lips trembled into a smile, her hand tightening around her gloves until the leather creaked. "You're here," she whispered. "You came back."

His smile was weary, but real. "Aye. For now."

Although the harbour still stank of oil and smoke, though the war was far from done, the sight of him standing before her was enough to make the world, for one fleeting instant, whole again.

The bustle of the quay slowly thinned. Sailors disappeared toward the barracks or into waiting lorries, Wrens drifted back to their posts, and the heavy ropes creaked as *Fury* settled against the stone.

They walked a little way along the quay, past the stacks of crates and the shadows of the sheds, until they were half hidden from view. His hand closed gently over hers.

Nancy turned to him, and the composure she had fought to hold since dawn crumbled. The relief came in a rush, tears burning her eyes as she pressed a hand against his chest, feeling the solid thrum of his heartbeat.

"You're really here," she whispered, her voice breaking. "I thought—" She couldn't finish.

Fred caught her close, his arms wrapping around her as though he could shield her from the whole war. "I know," he murmured against her hair. "I'm here, Nance. I came back."

She clung to him, letting the sob escape, muffled against his tunic. His uniform smelled of salt and oil, smoke and steel, but beneath it was something unmistakably him, and it steadied her.

For a long moment neither spoke, content just to hold and be held. Then, as she drew back slightly, Fred's hand lingered at her cheek, rough from salt and weather. His eyes, weary and shadowed, searched hers with quiet intensity.

"I don't know how many more times I'll get to come back," he said softly. "Just know every time I do… it's for you."

Nancy's breath hitched, her tears spilling into a smile. "Then I'll be here, every time."

The war still rumbled on beyond the harbour, but in that stolen corner of morning, they let themselves forget it.

For the first time in months, neither of them had a duty to rush to. The morning broke soft and cool, the harbour quiet except for the cry of gulls. Nancy waited by the gate in her best coat, nervous as a girl of seventeen, and when Fred appeared — cap tucked under his arm, tunic pressed, a smile tugging at the corner of his mouth — the world seemed to ease.

They walked into the village first, boots crunching along the lane, talking of everything and nothing. Fred bought them both barley sweets from a grocer's jar, and Nancy laughed when he handed her the largest one with a mock bow. She hadn't laughed so freely in years, and the sound startled even her.

The sun broke through at last, spilling gold across the harbour and the low green hills beyond. Light danced on the crest of the waves, each shimmer a promise that the world could still be beautiful, even here. The air carried a strange mingling — the salt sting of the sea, the faint sweetness of spring blossoms on the wind, and the ever-present undertone of oil and soot from the base. It should have clashed, but somehow it didn't. To Nancy, walking beside Fred, it felt like the truest reflection of the moment: war's shadow still close, yet threaded with warmth, with hope, with the impossible brightness of happiness she had almost forgotten could exist.

By midday they had wandered into the hills. The air was sharp with heather and peat smoke, the view stretching out to the grey sweep of the sea. Fred dropped onto the grass with a sigh, tugging at his collar. "Feels strange," he admitted, lying back against the slope. "To have a whole sky over me without scanning for planes."

Nancy sat beside him, knees tucked under her skirt, watching the wind ruffle his hair. "Feels strange to be here without static in my ears," she said softly.

He turned his head, smiling up at her. "Then we're both adrift together."

The afternoon passed unhurried. They picnicked on bread and cheese wrapped in paper, shared an orange that tasted of summer. Nancy found herself telling him about the grocer's shop where she'd worked before the war — the rows of sugar cones, the weighing scales that always stuck, the gossip of customers. Fred, in turn, told her about his first posting, a destroyer out of Plymouth, the way he'd been sick as a boy on his first patrol but refused to let anyone see.

"You? A lieutenant of His Majesty's Navy, reduced to clinging to the rail? I'd have paid good money to see it." Nancy mocked upon hearing Freds story.

"I'm sure I looked very dignified — pale as a ghost, swaying like a drunk, praying the sea would spit me out." Fred rolled his eyes, playing along with Nancy mocking him.

"Well, it makes you human at least. I half thought you were carved out of oak, the way you stand so straight." She raised her eyes unwittingly to consume him.

"I assure you; I'm far from oak. Closer to driftwood, most days." He returned the gaze, smiling back.

Nancy sat silent, studying him for a moment, before nudging him and responding:

"Driftwood doesn't steer convoys through the Atlantic. Nor does it write letters that make long nights feel shorter."

Fred's breath caught as he felt the playfulness fading into something more serious.

As the light began to fade, they wandered back towards the village, hand brushing against hand until Fred finally took hers properly. Neither spoke of tomorrow, or of the convoys that waited, or of the dangers pressing in on every side. For one day, they let themselves pretend that they were simply a man and a woman, walking home together as though peace already reigned.

Nancy held onto the warmth of his hand, the comforting weight of it, and thought fiercely: *I will remember this. Whatever comes, I will remember this.*

CARELESS TRUST

The air on the base grew warmer as spring took hold, however, with it came a sharper edge to duty. Rumours drifted in with the sea-mist—of spies uncovered in London, of coded transmissions intercepted nearby, of traitors who had passed secrets across the Channel. Posters warned them again and again: "Careless Talk Costs Lives." Nancy had always taken it as background noise before, but now the words seemed to look back at her with new weight. Careless talk. Careless trust. Who, she wandered, could afford either anymore?

Nancy rubbed her eyes, the wireless hiss droning in her ears. It was near midnight, the air heavy with fatigue, when something odd caught her attention. The transmission was routine — a merchant ship relaying its position — but when Nancy compared the figures to the chart, her brow furrowed. The coordinates were wrong. Not just wrong, but dangerously so. If the convoy followed them, they'd be miles off course, straight into waters known to be prowled by U-boats.

She double-checked the log. Someone had already written the message down, signed off, and passed it to the duty officer. The figures didn't match what she'd heard. Nancy's heart thudded. Either she had made a mistake — or someone else had deliberately altered the message.

The thought made her stomach twist. Inside this draughty hut, among women she shared tea and biscuits with, was it possible one of them was working against them?

Mary appeared at her shoulder. "You look like you've seen a ghost."

Nancy snapped the notebook shut. "It's nothing," she said too quickly. Her pulse however, told her it was everything.

The glare of several Wrens met Nancy. As she paced out of the hut, she could feel the burn of Iris Moffatts stare into her back.

Nancy pushed open the heavy door of the signals hut, blinking against the sudden brightness. After hours bent over the set, the sunshine struck her like a blessing, sharp and golden on her face. She paused on the step, drawing in a breath. The air smelled of salt and tar, with just the faintest hint of new grass from the hills beyond — spring trying to push its way through the ever-present shadow of war.

She tilted her head, letting the warmth soak into her skin. It was the same sun she and Fred had walked beneath only a few days ago, the same light that had caught in his hair, that had glinted on the waves while his hand rested steady in hers. Though he was gone now, back at sea, she knew with a certainty that defied reason that he was feeling it too. The same warmth. The same wind. A fragile thread stretched between them across the miles of water, binding them together under the same sky.

⚓

Nancy couldn't shake the thought of the altered message she had found in the log. She stood stiffly before Commander Talbot's desk, the logbook clutched to her chest. The room smelled faintly of tobacco and floor polish, the blinds drawn against the morning light. Talbot didn't look up at first, his pen scratching steadily across a form. When he finally did, his expression was cool, faintly irritated.

"Well, Carter? You insisted on seeing me."

Nancy opened the log, turning it toward him, her finger jabbing at the line of altered bearings. "Sir, I believe these were tampered with. If they'd have been passed on, the convoy would have been sent into danger. This isn't the first irregularity I've noticed. There was the fire in the hut, the log with the incorrect bearings, the cut cable—"

Talbot held up a hand, frowning. "Enough. You're suggesting sabotage?"

"Yes, sir," Nancy said, her voice trembling but firm. "I am."

Silence stretched between them as time seemed to stop in its tracks. Talbot's eyes bore into hers, his mouth set in a thin line. Then he leaned back in his chair, exhaling smoke from the pipe he'd just lit.

"Carter, I know these long watches strain the nerves. You girls work hard — too hard sometimes — and it's easy to see patterns where none exist. A blown fuse, a sloppy log entry, a smudge of ink… hardly the work of Hitler's spies."

Nancy's chest tightened. "With respect, sir, this is more than a smudge. Lives have been lost with incorrect information. If I'm right—"

"You're not," he cut in sharply, snapping the log shut and pushing it back across the desk. "And if you value your place here, I'd advise you not to spread tales. We've enough trouble without paranoia undermining morale."

Heat burned Nancy's cheeks. She wanted to argue, to plead, but the weight of his stare pinned her tongue. Slowly, she gathered the log and saluted, her hand shaking.

"Dismissed," Talbot said, already bending back to his paperwork.

Nancy left the office with her stomach twisting. Outside, the gulls wheeled over the harbour, their cries shrill in the wind. Talbot might dismiss her fears, but she knew what she had seen. Something was wrong at this base — and if no one else would act, perhaps it would fall to her.

The dormitory smelled faintly of damp wool and lavender soap, the air heavy with the quiet breathing of girls already asleep. Nancy sat on the edge of her bunk, boots unlaced, staring at the floorboards. The logbook lay hidden beneath her pillow, as if keeping it close might keep the truth from slipping away.

Mary slid in beside her, hair loose around her shoulders, eyes shadowed with fatigue. "Well?" she whispered. "You saw him, didn't you? What did Talbot say?"

Nancy's throat tightened. "He dismissed it. Called me paranoid. Said I was seeing patterns where there aren't any."

Mary let out a long breath, her face falling. "Oh, Nance." She reached for her hand, giving it a quick squeeze. "Then you've got to drop it. Please. For your own sake."

Nancy turned to her, stung. "You think I imagined it too?"

"No," Mary said quickly. "I think you're sharp-eyed. Too sharp, sometimes. If Talbot won't listen, and if word gets around you're pressing this—" She shook her head. "People will turn on you. You've heard the whispers already."

Nancy swallowed hard, the weight of it heavy in her chest. Mary's hand was warm in hers, her eyes wide with worry.

"I can't just ignore it," Nancy whispered back. "If there's someone here working against us—"

Mary's grip tightened, fierce. "Then let someone else find them. You've carried enough, Nance. Don't let this drag you under."

Nancy nodded faintly, but inside the fire only burned hotter. She knew what she'd seen, and no amount of dismissal, no amount of whispered warnings, could convince her otherwise.

TRAINING TIME

Fred leaned against the cold steel, the sunlight glinting on the restless water. For once, the sea lay calm, the destroyer sliding through the swell with an ease that felt almost unnatural after months of grey gales and wolfpacks. The men joked on deck, stripped to shirtsleeves as they drilled, their laughter carrying in the wind. On the surface, it was just another exercise. Everyone knew this training was different. The scale, the secrecy — everyone felt it weighing on them, it could only mean one thing.

Fred hadn't told Nancy. He didn't have to. She would have known, the way she always seemed to know. He pictured her face in that spring sunlight, the warmth of her hand in his, the way the air had smelled of blossom threaded with salt and smoke. The same sun touched him now, fierce and bright, but here at sea the wind bit sharper, salted spray stinging his lips.

Still, when he closed his eyes, it was the same sun. The same warmth. He carried it with him, as if part of her had followed him aboard. In that moment, even with the weight of what was to come, he felt almost whole.

The mess deck smelled of tea and the faint tang of oil that clung to everything aboard. Hammocks swung lazily overhead, crammed so close that a man could barely roll over without jostling his neighbour. A battered gramophone sat in the corner, its needle worn to nothing, but the boys coaxed music from it all the same — scratchy dance tunes that reminded them of home.

They were young, most of them barely shaving. Yet hardened already by endless watches. The older hands teased them mercilessly, but always with a kind of rough fondness. They shared cigarettes, swapped stories, carved initials into the wooden tables when the officers weren't looking.

In quieter moments, the laughter thinned and the fear showed. Some wrote letters, hunched over scraps of paper, their faces tight as they searched for words. Others sat silent, staring at nothing, their mugs of tea cooling in their hands. The sea pressed in on them always — above, below, around — and each man knew how quickly steel could tear, how fast the cold could kill.

The men all knew this wasn't ordinary convoy duty. The drills were longer, harsher, every exercise repeated until their muscles burned. They practiced lowering landing craft in rough seas, gunnery against towed targets, damage control until their knuckles bled. No one said the word invasion aloud, but it hung in the air like the tang of cordite. They joked to keep the edge off — calling it "the big show" or "Jerry's party" — but their eyes betrayed them when the laughter faded. Each man understood they were rehearsing for something greater than they'd ever faced, and though they never admitted it, they were terrified.

Yet when the call came — "Action stations!" — they moved as one. Boots hammered on steel, hands flying to stations they could find blindfolded. Fear became focus. The depth charge crews grinned through clenched teeth as they heaved the fat cylinders into place, pretending not to think of what — or who — might be waiting beneath.

"Come on, lads, shift yourselves!" Chief Petty Officer Dobson bellowed as two stokers wrestled with a length of hose for the hundredth time that morning. "Jerry's not going to wait politely while you get your knickers untangled!"

The men groaned, sweat soaking through their shirts despite the sharp wind. One of the stokers, a wiry boy from Liverpool, shot back between gritted teeth: "If Jerry sees me in knickers, Chief, he'll drop dead of shock and save us the trouble."

The mess deck erupted with laughter, even as they heaved the hose into place. Someone banged a spanner against the bulkhead in applause.

"Less talking, more working!" Dobson barked, though his mouth twitched at the corners.

Nearby, the gunnery team were lining up on a towed target, the younger lads squinting into the spray. "Bet you a week's pay I can hit it first shot," one of them boasted.

"You haven't hit anything since Portsmouth, you daft sod," another responded. "Best keep your pay for buying me a pint when we get leave."

Fred, watching from the bridge, felt the corners of his own mouth tug upward. Their laughter rang false sometimes, a little too loud, but he welcomed it. Better laughter than silence. Better banter than the creeping edge of fear.

Fred watched them with fixated eyes, pride and dread tangled in his chest. These were his boys, his responsibility. Although he kept his voice even, his orders clipped, he carried their faces with him long after the ship fell quiet again.

The whistle shrilled across the deck, sharp and urgent. Boots beat on steel as men scrambled into position, each one clutching a line, a tool, or a rifle. Fred stood at the bridge rail, watching the crew pour into their stations. It wasn't battle, not yet—but the drill was meant to feel like it.

"Action stations! Action stations!" The boatswain's voice carried down the length of the destroyer. Hatches slammed, metal on metal, as compartments were sealed.

The new lads still moved with the jitter of inexperience. One boy, no older than nineteen, fumbled with the breech of a deck gun, nearly dropping the heavy shell. The petty officer beside him barked, "Faster! In action you'll have seconds, not minutes!" The boy's hands shook, but he steadied, fed the round home, and locked the mechanism.

The ship itself seemed to come alive—engines rumbling deeper, turbines winding up as if eager for speed. A shrill ring of the engine-room telegraph echoed up through the deck plates. Somewhere below, stokers sweated in the heat, shovelling coal dust from the bilges or tending valves, lungs stung by steam.

Fred moved between stations, correcting, encouraging, reminding the men of the rhythm: eyes on the horizon, ears open for the next order, hands quick but precise. The destroyer lived and died by discipline. A single mistake in action—a jammed gun, a missed bearing—could be the end of all of them.

"Port lookout!" he called. "Report!"

"Clear, sir!"

"Starboard?"

"Clear, sir!"

It was all rehearsal, but the crew's faces told another story. Sweat ran down temples, knuckles whitened on ropes and rails. Every man knew that tomorrow—or the day after—these same drills might be the only thing standing between them and a torpedo in the belly.

The final blast of the whistle ended the exercise. Orders to stand down rang out, and the crew let out a collective breath. Laughter, nervous and thin, rippled along the deck. The young seaman at the gun wiped his brow, trying to look as though he hadn't been trembling moments earlier.

Fred allowed himself the faintest of smiles. The destroyer wasn't perfect yet, but she was sharpening. When the real test came, he would need them ready—every man, every station, drilled until instinct carried them through the smoke and fire.

The days blurred with drills aboard Fury. At dawn, gunnery practice rattled the decks, the bark of the four-inch guns echoing across the grey water. By mid-morning the crew were running fire drills, dragging hoses through narrow passageways, smoke candles filling the compartments until eyes stung and throats burned. After that came damage-control exercises—shoring up bulkheads, sealing watertight doors, hammering home wedges until their arms ached. Every man knew his station, every movement becoming instinct, until the ship herself seemed to move with them.

Fred wiped a streak of sweat from his brow, sloping against the handrail as the whistle blew to stand down. Beside him, Jack Curzon was shaking his head, the grin on his face not quite masking his fatigue.

"They're working us like it's doomsday," Jack muttered, flexing his shoulders. "Never known so many drills in one stretch. Half the lads reckon the officers are trying to kill us before the Jerries do."

Fred gave a quiet huff of laughter but didn't quite smile. "It's more than that. Feels… sharper.

Like we're being readied for something. These aren't just routine drills."

Jack shot him a sidelong glance. "You and your gut feelings. What d'you think it is then?"

Fred's eyes drifted out over the endless swell, the convoy plodding ahead of them in neat grey columns. "I don't know," he admitted. "But the way they're pushing us, it feels like the calm before something bigger. One last convoy, then… who knows."

Jack snorted, though his gaze followed Fred's out to sea. "Well, whatever it is, we'll be ready. *Fury's* never been sharper." He thumped the rail with the flat of his hand, but the weight in his tone betrayed his own unease.

Fred nodded, but the thought lingered, heavy as the sea itself. The drills weren't just drills anymore. They were preparation. Although no one would say it aloud, he could feel it in his bones—something was coming.

UNDER ATTACK

For Fred, the days of U-boat hunting blurred into a taut, exhausting routine. The Atlantic was endless—grey sea, grey sky, the horizon swallowed in mist—and yet every inch of it felt dangerous. At the wheel or on lookout, he never allowed his gaze to soften, never let his mind drift. Somewhere out there, beneath the rolling swells, the wolfpacks hunted them in silence.

The asdic's steady ping echoed through the hull, a sound Fred had come to dread. Each pulse thudded like a heartbeat, filling the mess decks, reminding them all that they were searching, searching, always searching. And when the cry of

"Contact!" rang out, the ship jolted into frantic motion. Orders barked, engines roaring, men rushing to their stations. Fred's hands clenched around the wheel as the destroyer swung hard, spray whipping across the bow, depth charges rolled into the sea. Moments later the ocean erupted—thunderous blasts sending shudders through steel, through bone, as black water foamed and hissed astern.

Fred would lean with the others over the railing, squinting at the boiling wake. Sometimes there was wreckage—a splinter of wood, an oil slick spreading dark on the surface. More often, there was nothing. Silence returned, heavier than before, leaving the question gnawing at them all: had they struck true, or had the U-boat slipped away, ready to stalk them again in the night?

Wolfpacks were worse still. The tension doubled when the signals came in—two, three, even four U-boats shadowing the convoy, striking under cover of darkness. Fred would stand his watch in the pitch black, nerves raw, listening for the sudden bark of guns or the boom of torpedoes hitting home. He had seen merchantmen vanish in sheets of flame, their crews scrambling in lifeboats or into the cold Atlantic. Fury tore through the swell, guns barking, searchlights sweeping, depth charges roaring, but still the shadows lingered.

It was a kind of hunting that never felt like victory. Each chase left Fred drained, his stomach knotted, and though he told himself they were the hunters, deep down he knew—they were prey too, and the wolfpacks were always waiting.

The sea was steel-grey that morning, still like a mill-pond, the horizon lost in a low mist that blurred sky and water into one endless sheet of iron. Fred stood at the bow of the destroyer, thinking of the recent training, the plans laid out ahead, and watched the convoy form up. The last convoy run before the plans unfold.

The days at sea blurred into a steady rhythm of duty and endurance. Stokers fed coal and oil into the hungry boilers below, stripped to their undershirts in the sweltering heat while the ship's deck shivered with each turn of the screws. On the mess deck, men hunched over enamel mugs of tea, playing cards with battered packs, their laughter too loud to hide the edge of nerves. Others coiled ropes, chipped rust from the railings, or scrubbed the salt from steel with stiff brushes until their hands blistered. The gunners ran drills on their weapons, swinging barrels back and forth until the movement became muscle memory, while lookouts scanned the endless horizon, eyes stinging from wind and spray. There was always work: splicing ropes, greasing machinery, checking depth charge rails. Even in the rare quiet hours, hammocks swayed tight in the cramped mess, boots tucked into the netting above, and the air smelled of oil, sea salt and tobacco. The sea was never still, and neither were they.

Dozens of merchant ships plodded into position, black silhouettes chugging stubbornly westward. They were laden with food, fuel, munitions — lifelines Britain could not survive without. Each one was a fat, lumbering target.

Around them, the escort screen fell into place — destroyers and corvettes cutting sharp arcs through the swell, their presence both reassuring and woefully inadequate. Fred knew too well how thin the line was between safety and slaughter.

The air smelled of oil and salt. Somewhere deep in the fog, a gull cried, then was lost to the thrum of engines.

The captain's voice carried across the deck: "Convoy WS-49. Course west by north-west. Maintain formation."

Fred tightened his grip on the rail. Every instinct told him the danger was coming. The North Atlantic was too quiet. Too still.

He thought of Nancy. She would be at her post in Scotland, headphones pressed tight, pencil scratching across her logbook. He could almost hear her voice in the whisper of the wind: Be careful, Fred. Keep your eyes open.

He forced the image aside. War gave no room for sentiment, not here. Out in the mist, beneath the waves, he could almost feel them waiting — the wolves, silent, patient, already scenting their prey.

The convoy sailed on, unaware.

A ripple of unease ran through the deck. The lookouts shifted in their stations, peering into the fog, hands tightening on binoculars. Somewhere astern, a ship's whistle sounded, long and low, the sound smothered by the mist.

"Sonar reports contact!" The shout snapped like a whip across the bridge.

Fred's pulse kicked. He straightened, eyes fixed on the grey nothingness ahead. The captain's orders followed fast — crisp, hard. "Action stations. Bring her about."

The klaxon shrieked. Boots thundered on steel, men racing to their posts. Depth charges were primed, the gunners swinging their weapons to cover the convoy's flanks. The destroyer heeled sharply as she turned, the fog tearing across her deck in ragged veils.

Fred braced against the capstan, jaw tight. The stillness had broken. Somewhere below them, a periscope eye was already watching, already calculating.

In that moment, he thought again of Nancy — her voice, bold and calm, cutting through the static. He clung to it like a talisman as the first charge tumbled into the sea, the thunder rolling back through the ship.

The wolves had arrived.

The deck shuddered as another depth charge went over the stern, the blast rolling up through Fred's boots. Spray lashed across the rails, men shouting as the destroyer heeled hard to port. Somewhere out in the fog, a freighter's siren wailed, followed by the dull boom of an explosion.

Fred caught sight of Seaman Harris — barely more than a boy, freckles stark against his pale face — fumbling with the primer on a depth charge. His hands shook so badly the pin slipped twice from his grip.

"Steady, lad!" Fred barked, crossing the deck in three strides. He clamped a hand on the boy's shoulder, firm but not unkind. "Breathe. One thing at a time. You know this drill better than you think."

Harris's eyes were wide, panicked. "Sir—they're all around us. I can feel it. We'll never—"

"Look at me." Fred's voice cut sharp, calm as steel. Harris met his gaze, chest heaving. Fred lowered his tone, steady, deliberate. "We've trained for this. You do your part, the next man does his, and we'll see them off. You understand? No panic. Not on my deck."

The boy swallowed hard, then nodded, forcing his shaking fingers to steady as he slid the primer into place.

"That's it," Fred said quietly, giving his shoulder a brief squeeze. "Good lad. Now keep at it. You'll give Jerry something to think about yet."

A fresh blast shook the sea astern, the spray towering high as the charges detonated. The destroyer surged forward again, engines roaring. Fred turned back toward the bridge, his jaw clenched, his own pulse racing. He couldn't let the boy see his fear. Couldn't let any of them see it.

A lookout's cry tore through the mist: "Torpedo wake! Port side!"

Fred spun toward the sound, heart in his throat. Through the grey veil he saw it — a pale streak slicing the water, arrowing straight for the fat hull of a tanker lumbering at the convoy's edge.

"Signal her to turn!" the captain shouted from the bridge. But, the warning came too late.

The torpedo struck midships with a muffled crack that turned to a thunderclap. A column of fire leapt skyward, orange against the fog, the tanker's belly ripping open. Men spilled from her deck like ants shaken from a hive, their cries piercing even over the roar of the explosion.

On the destroyer's deck, silence fell for a heartbeat — sailors frozen, eyes wide as they watched the inferno consume the ship.

Fred's voice snapped them back to their duty. "Back to stations! Eyes on your gear!" He grabbed Harris, who had gone rigid, staring at the burning hulk. "Don't look, lad. Do your job. We can't help them now."

Harris swallowed hard, tearing his gaze away, fumbling again at the depth charge rack. Around them, the crew moved with jerky precision, forcing themselves back to drills, each man fighting the instinct to watch the slaughter.

The tanker groaned as her bow sagged, her stern rising from the water. Flames crackled along spilled fuel, the smoke thick and choking even at a distance. Fred gripped the rail until his knuckles whitened, forcing his voice firm and calm as he called orders.

"Keep her sweeping! Charges ready aft!"

He didn't let his men see the tremor in his hand. Didn't let them see the guilt gnawing inside — that he was still standing on steel while those poor devils flailed in the fire.

The sea swallowed the vessel with a hiss, leaving only burning slicks and scattered men fighting for their lives. The convoy closed ranks, steaming grimly on.

Fred drew a sharp breath, his jaw set. There would be time enough later for grief. For now, he could only keep his ship afloat — and pray to whatever powers the sea obeyed that Nancy would never hear his voice break.

Hours later, the calm was restored. Fred couldn't help wonder, how this could have happened. This was a clear route. The communications had been confident. He wrestled the thoughts before storming into the communications centre and demanding contact to relay the message.

INTERROGATION

The room was small, the windows shuttered, the air thick with smoke. A single lamp swung slightly overhead, its circle of light falling across the table where Nancy sat. Her hands were folded tightly in her lap, though she kept willing them not to tremble.

Opposite her, two officers leaned forward — Commander Briggs, with his clipped moustache and sharper tongue, and Lieutenant Harvey, who hadn't spoken yet but whose eyes never left her face.

Briggs dropped the signal sheet onto the table with a snap. "Miss Carter, this is your handwriting, is it not?"

Nancy nodded. "Yes, sir. That's not what I copied from the wireless. Someone altered it after—"

"Altered?" Briggs cut her off. "Or deliberately written incorrectly?"

Her heart lurched. "No! I swear, sir, I transcribed what I heard. The numbers were different."

Harvey finally spoke, voice quiet but carrying. "You were on duty when three separate signals contained errors that could have compromised an entire convoy."

Nancy felt heat rush to her cheeks. "Because someone is tampering with them! I tried to report it, but—"

Briggs slammed a hand against the table, making her flinch. "You realise the gravity of this? If you are withholding information, if you are lying…" He let the words trail off, the implication heavy.

Nancy forced herself to sit straighter, though her stomach twisted. "I'm not lying. I've given everything I can to this base. I've lost people too — don't you dare question my loyalty." Her voice cracked on the last word, but she didn't look away.

The silence stretched. The ticking of a clock filled the room, unbearably loud.

At last, Harvey leaned back in his chair, studying her. "If you're telling the truth, Miss Carter, then someone very close to you is not. Be certain you want to pursue this."

Nancy's throat felt dry, but she nodded. She thought of Fred at sea, of the convoys under threat, of Edward's name carved into the village memorial. "I want the truth," she whispered. "Whatever it costs."

Nancy headed back to the bunk after being dismissed, replaying the words, seeing only the strict faces for Briggs and Harvey sat across from her. The scolding. Why her? Nancy thought in silent. She was the one raising the alarms, noticing the patterns, bringing them to attention, her thoughts spiraled.

The barracks smelled faintly of coal smoke and lavender polish. Nancy pushed open the door to the shared dormitory, her shoulders aching with exhaustion from the interrogation. She wanted nothing more than to collapse into her bunk, draw the blanket over her head, and forget the world outside.

The room fell silent the moment she entered. Conversations that had been buzzing moments before cut off mid-sentence. A couple of Wrens glanced at her, then quickly looked away. Someone coughed.

Nancy's heart sank. They knew. Or at least, they'd heard the rumours.

Mary was sitting cross-legged on her bed, mending a stocking under the dim yellow light. She didn't look up straight away, and when she did, her smile was faint, strained.

"You're late back," Mary said lightly, too lightly.

Nancy sat on the edge of her own bunk, struggling to find her voice. "They kept me in. Questions."

Mary's hands stilled on the needle. "That's what they're saying. That you… that it was your log sheets."

Nancy whipped her head up, anger flaring. "You don't believe that, do you?"

Mary hesitated — too long. The pause was worse than words.

"I don't know what to believe, Nance," she admitted softly. "Three errors, all on your watch? It looks bad. And they said…" She trailed off, shaking her head. "You've been distracted lately. You write letters all the time. To that naval officer. Maybe someone thinks—"

"That I'd betray my country for Fred?" Nancy snapped, her voice louder than she intended. The others in the room shifted uncomfortably, pretending not to listen but clearly hanging on every word.

Mary's eyes filled with something Nancy couldn't bear to name — doubt, or worse, pity. "I just… I don't want you to get hurt. If you've been set up, if someone's using you, then you need to be careful."

Nancy's throat tightened. For months, Mary had been her anchor, her laughter in the dull hours, her confidante. Now, it seemed, even Mary wasn't sure.

She rose abruptly, turning towards the door. "If you don't trust me, Mary, then you don't know me at all."

The door shut behind her with a hollow thud, leaving the room in heavy silence.

Out in the cold night air, Nancy drew in a shaky breath. The sea wind stung her eyes, but she didn't wipe them. Somewhere out there, Fred was fighting to survive. Here, she was fighting a different kind of battle — one that struck deeper than torpedoes or bombs.

TRAITOR

The hut buzzed with the low hum of voices and the crackle of static, but Nancy's blood ran cold as she rifled through the intercept drawer again. The folder was gone. She'd checked it the night before, locked it in its place with her own hand — a full set of intercepts flagged urgent, chatter about wolfpacks converging in the North Atlantic. Now, with the morning shift, it had vanished.

She stood frozen, fingers trembling over the neat rows of files. "Mary," she hissed, "did you move last night's intercepts?"

Mary shook her head, frowning. "No. Why?"

Nancy snapped the drawer shut, her pulse hammering. This wasn't a misplaced slip or a smudge in the logs. This was deliberate.

Nancy paused. Her face wore deep contemplation, so much so, Mary didn't question again. Nancy poured through the next step. *Going direct to Talbot is the right thing to do. But if he doesn't believe me again…* Nancy thoughts twisted. *Perhaps I go to Elsie again… or another commander. Going around Talbot could lead to Court Martial. Is it worth the risk?*

After weighing the risks, she hurried to Talbot's office, not waiting for permission to enter. Commander Talbot was a tall, spare man in his fifties, with thinning iron-grey hair and a neatly kept moustache that did little to soften the stern lines of his face. His uniform was immaculate, pressed to regulation perfection, though his eyes — pale and sharp as flint — suggested nothing escaped his notice. He carried himself with the stiff-backed bearing of a career officer, a man shaped by the Navy long before this war, his presence commanding respect even before he spoke. He looked up sharply from his desk, annoyance flashing — until he saw her face.

"Carter?"

She thrust the empty folder onto his desk, her voice taut. "Gone, sir. An entire set of intercepts. I locked them away myself. If they don't reach Command, a convoy will sail blind, likely straight into danger."

Talbot's jaw tightened. For a moment he said nothing, only leaned back, eyes narrowing. Then he rose, crossed to the door, and turned the key in the lock.

"Tell me everything," he said quietly.

Nancy's breath caught. This was different. The dismissal, the patronising smile — gone. In its place was something hard, sharp, and alert.

She steadied her voice. "This isn't the first time, sir. The altered bearings, the fire, the cut cable. I've tried to tell you. Someone here is tampering with our work."

Talbot's gaze flicked to the empty folder again, his lips pressed thin. "And now they've gone too far."

For the first time, Nancy saw the faintest crack in his composure — not disbelief, but concern.

He picked up the folder, weighing it as though it might tell him where it had gone.

"You'll say nothing of this outside this room," he ordered. "Not to your friends, not to your bunkmates. Do you understand?"

"Yes, sir," Nancy whispered, her heart racing.

Talbot met her eyes, his expression grave. "Then we have a traitor in this base, and we'll smoke them out."

Nancy stepped out of Commander Talbot's office with her chin lifted just a fraction higher, the echo of his grudging words still ringing in her ears. At last, he had agreed— *"We'll smoke them out."* She felt the tight coil in her chest loosen, replaced by a fierce satisfaction that warmed her through more than the draughty corridor ever could. For weeks she had carried suspicion alone, doubted by her peers and dismissed as obsessive, but now her instincts had weight, her voice authority. As the door clicked shut behind her, she allowed herself the smallest of smiles. The traitor thought themselves clever, hidden in the hum of static and signals—but Nancy Carter had just set the trap.

Sound in the knowledge that Talbot had understood her words, Nancy was not reeling in victory, but from the sting that even here, even among fellow comrades, betrayal was possible. Nancy headed back into the hut, where she noticed Harvey stood at the edge of the signals room, posture too casual, his gaze darting now and then toward the logbooks. When spoken to, he replied promptly enough, yet there was often a faint delay, as if he'd been pulled from thoughts elsewhere. Nancy thought about the time she once caught him smoothing the page of a ledger long after he'd written in it, fingers hovering a fraction too long over the entry. Nancy reflected on some of the odd behaviors she had witnessed, coincidences. Perhaps. She recalled she had seen him slip a folded note into his pocket with a glance so quick it almost escaped notice. Nothing concrete, nothing she could pin down—but each moment left her unsettled, her mind circling back to him long after, pondering the thoughts of coincidence, or something more…

NO PEACE IN WAR

Nancy unfolded the letter slowly, recognising her mother's careful hand at once. The familiar loops and slants of the writing were like a voice carried across the miles, and for a moment, the barracks and the war fell away.

Dearest Nancy,

You'll be glad to know the garden is keeping us well enough. The hens are still laying, though not as often, and your father has turned half the meadow over to potatoes. It's strange to think how life revolves around rations now—queueing for hours, counting every ounce of butter, making one tin of jam last a month. We all make do, of course. Your Aunt Mirium knitted socks for the Home Guard and we've been sharing out what little we have with neighbours. The spirit of it keeps us going.

Nancy smiled faintly as she read, her heart tugging at the picture of the village continuing on in its quiet resilience. Then her eyes caught on the next lines, and her breath caught.

We have taken in two girls—one a Jewish refugee from Germany. Martha, and Edna, an evacuee from London. They are small things, Martha is as thin as rails, but bright-eyed, and already calling this place "home." They both follow your father about the farm as if he were a general and laugh when he tries to teach them to milk a cow. They've lost so much, yet they smile when the hens cluck and chase them, or when the church bells sound on Sunday. We feel blessed to have them here, to give them safety, even with all the hardship.

Nancy pressed the page to her chest, overcome with a swell of pride and ache. Her family, still in the quiet Cheshire countryside, were part of something larger than themselves—opening their door to the displaced, carrying on the small, stubborn work of survival. It brought the war home to her in another way: not just through convoys and raids, but in the faces of children who had lost everything.

Nancy lowered the letter slowly, her fingers brushing the paper as though reluctant to put it down. Mary, sitting cross-legged on the bunk opposite, tilted her head.

"Good news?" she asked gently.

Nancy nodded, though her voice caught. "From home. They've taken in two girls— a Jewish refugee from Germany, and an evacuee from the city. Martha and Edna." She gave a small smile, eyes distant as she spoke. "Thin as twigs, but already chasing the hens round the yard. Mum says they laugh at everything, even when there's nothing to laugh about. I can almost see it… the meadow, the hens, those girls trailing after my father as if he were the king himself."

Mary's lips curved softly, though her eyes glistened. "That's good of them. To give those girls a place. Must make you proud."

"It does," Nancy murmured, pressing the folded letter to her chest again. "Proud, and homesick all at once. They've so little, and yet they share it without a thought."

For a moment the two women sat in quiet, the weight of it lingering between them. Then the duty bell clanged from down the corridor, its sharp ring breaking the stillness.

Mary stood, brushing down her skirt with a sigh. "That'll be our shift."

Nancy tucked the letter carefully into her pocket, letting her fingers rest there a moment longer. "Back to the signals, then."

Side by side, they left the barracks, the sound of their boots quickening against the stone floor as they returned to the endless clatter of typewriters and the crackle of voices carried through the static.

The door to the signals hut creaked open and Elsie stepped inside, the usual light in her face extinguished. Her eyes were red raw, her cheeks puffed and blotched from crying, though no sound came from her now. In her hand she clutched a crumpled letter, the paper trembling faintly with each shallow breath she drew. She stood frozen in the doorway, unable to move further, as though crossing the threshold would make the words she carried all the more real.

The room fell silent around her, the low chatter and rustle of papers dying away at once. No one needed to ask—her grief spoke more loudly than words could. The letter told her all that mattered: her husband's bomber had not returned from its raid. Somewhere out there, in the dark sky over Europe, he had vanished with his crew, swallowed by the war.

Elsie's fingers clenched tighter around the page, knuckles white, as she stared into the room without truly seeing it. Her friends rose quietly, moving toward her, but still she did not speak. The world had shifted in the space of a single letter, and she stood at the edge of it, unmoored.

Mary was the first to move, crossing the hut with a gentleness that seemed to still the air. She laid a hand on Elsie's arm, her voice soft, barely more than a whisper. "Come and sit down, love."

Elsie didn't answer, but she allowed herself to be guided to a bench, the letter still clutched in her fist as though prising it away would undo the last link to him. Nancy sat on her other side, close enough that their shoulders touched, offering comforting presence where words failed.

Around them the other Wrens gathered, quiet, subdued. No one tried to say it would be alright—they all knew it wouldn't. Instead, small gestures filled the silence: a clean handkerchief pressed into Elsie's hand, a flask of tea slid across the table, a palm resting lightly on her back.

At last, Elsie's composure cracked. A shuddering sob broke free, followed by another, and she bent forward, pressing the letter to her lips as if she could still catch his scent on the paper. Mary wrapped her arms around her, holding her firmly, whispering small, steady words that could not mend but might at least hold her together for now.

Nancy blinked against the sting in her own eyes, reaching out to cover Elsie's hand with her own. The hut was hushed save for Elsie's grief, and in that silence every girl present felt the shadow of it settle over them—the knowledge that any letter, on any day, could bear the same cruel truth.

Pushing aside the horrible rumours, the whispers that always rose in the wake of loss, the girls closed ranks around Elsie. There was no talk of "what ifs" or speculation about the raid, only a quiet solidarity that bound them all together. Shoulders brushed, hands linked, hearts steadying against one another in silent promise. For Elsie, they would stand as one.

Yet for Nancy, the weight of it pressed harder with each passing minute. The air in the hut seemed close, the walls creeping in as though the grief had thickened them. She could hardly breathe for the heaviness of it—the realisation that no letter, no day, was ever safe. It was as if the sorrow that Elsie bore now seeped into every corner, whispering that tomorrow it could just as easily be her. The solidarity gave comfort to Elsie, but for Nancy it was suffocating, a reminder of how fragile her own moments of relief truly were.

⚓

Nancy slipped out of the barracks as the afternoon shadows lengthened, her steps quick over the cobbles. The air outside was sharp, carrying the tang of the sea, and she drank it in like a tonic after the suffocating closeness of the signals hut. The village was quiet, shopfronts lined with their stiff blackout curtains, the harbour clock ticking solemnly above the rooftops. She turned down the narrow lane and pushed open the door of the little tea shop.

The warmth inside wrapped around her at once, the rattle of crockery and the low murmur of conversation soft against her ears. She ordered her brew and found a small table by the window, where the pale autumn light fell across the worn wooden surface. The first sip steadied her, but it was the memory that came with it that eased her chest most of all: Fred, sitting opposite her not so long ago, his cap tucked under his arm, the faint smile he'd worn as he teased her for taking too much sugar. She could almost hear the echo of his laugh, feel the gentle brush of his hand across the table.

Nancy cradled the mug between her palms, staring into the steam as though it might conjure him there beside her. The tea shop hadn't changed—the same chipped saucers, the same lace curtains at the windows—but everything else had. Still, in that quiet moment, it was as if time folded in on itself, and she let herself remember, if only to escape the weight of the present.

Nancy cupped the mug tighter, the warmth seeping into her hands, but the comfort of it only deepened the hollow ache inside her. The memory of Fred across the table—his laugh, the light in his eyes—stung rather than soothed. She wished, with a pang so sharp it almost hurt to breathe, that their last words here had been lighter, filled with talk of futures rather than shadows of the past and present.

Her mind drifted, aching for a life they had only half-dared to dream aloud. A quiet house in the country, far from barracks and orders, where mornings would be broken by birdsong instead of bugles. She pictured a puppy tumbling in the garden, Fred's hands in the earth pulling weeds, laughter echoing from the kitchen as fresh bread cooled on the windowsill. A family, simple joys, normality—the kind of future the war seemed determined to keep out of reach.

Nancy blinked hard, staring down into her tea as though the swirling steam might carry her there. The ache sat heavy in her chest, a longing not just for

Fred, but for the life that waited beyond the end of all this, if only fate would allow them to grasp it.

The soft image in her mind—sunlit garden, puppy running in the grass, Fred's laughter on the breeze—shattered as a flicker of movement caught her eye. Out of the corner of her vision she saw Harvey, one of the senior officers, hunched at a table near the back of the tea room. He leaned in close to another man Nancy didn't recognise, their heads almost touching, words exchanged in low, hurried whispers.

Something about the way he held himself made her stomach tighten. Harvey wasn't laughing or sharing gossip over a pot of tea—his shoulders were stiff, his expression drawn, and he glanced toward the door more than once as though anxious to be seen. It was odd, out of place, and deeply unsettling. Nancy looked down quickly, pretending to fuss with her cup, though her heart gave a nervous flutter. The picture-perfect dream had slipped away, replaced instead with a cold unease that she couldn't quite explain.

SMOKE THEM OUT

The days blurred into one another, the weight of suspicion hanging like smoke over the hut. Though Talbot had given his word to "let her be," Nancy could still feel the doubt in the air, as though every scratch of her pencil was being measured against an invisible standard. Conversations hushed when she entered a room, and although no one spoke her name aloud, she could sense it perched on the edge of every silence.

She told herself she was used to silence — the long, crackling kind that filled her headphones, the silence of waiting for voices that might never come.

This was different, this silence pressed in close, watchful, heavy. Even Mary's chatter couldn't quite banish it, although she tried with relentless cheer, slipping jokes and gossip into the smallest gaps, determined to lift Nancy out of her thoughts.

At night, lying awake in the narrow bunk, Nancy turned Fred's letter over and over in her hands. The words had been read so often they were etched into her memory, yet she clung to them all the same, her shield against the gnawing question: what if the whispers were true? What if the doubt reached across the sea and tarnished his faith in her too?

Beyond the hut, preparations stirred. Rumours ran through the base like sparks — talk of landings, of the largest fleet ever assembled, of something vast about to break. Nancy felt it in her bones, the way the air seemed charged, restless. Fred's destroyer would be among them, she knew. Each tick of the clock brought him closer to the fire. Nancy, with her headphones and her pencil, could only listen, wait, and pray that when the storm came, he would find a way through.

Somewhere, out on the sea, Nancy knew Fred would be on his last convoy escort duty, before joining the largest fleet ever assembled.

⚓

The blackout had wrapped the base in silence. Only the low rumble of the generator broke the stillness as Nancy slipped into the signals hut, heart pounding. She wasn't supposed to be here tonight, but after weeks of doubt and whispers, after Mary's hesitation and the officers' suspicion, she needed proof.

She froze, silent, in the doorway.

At the far end of the room, a figure bent over the wireless, hands moving quickly, deliberately altering a set of coordinates in the logbook. The lamplight caught the gleam of spectacles — Lieutenant Harvey.

Her breath caught. Harvey, the quiet one, the officer who had sat across from her during the interrogation, who had asked her, *"Be certain you want to pursue this."*

Now she understood why.

Nancy's pulse thundered in her ears. She stepped forward, her boots loud on the floorboards. "Sir?"

Harvey jerked up, eyes wide behind the lenses. For a moment, his composure cracked. Then he straightened, closing the book with deliberate calm. "Miss Carter. You shouldn't be here."

Nancy forced steel into her voice. "You're the one changing the signals. It was you all along."

A flicker of a smile touched his lips, cold and sharp. "You're shrewder than they gave you credit for. A pity."

Her throat went dry. She could almost feel Edward's memory at her back, urging her not to falter, not to let this moment slip. She swallowed hard.

"You cost lives. Men are dead because of you."

His eyes glinted. "War is a messy thing. Not all victories are won at sea. Sometimes they're won with a pencil."

The words chilled her. She edged closer to the desk, desperate to get to the logbook. Harvey moved first, slamming it shut and tucking it under his arm.

Before she could react, the door burst open. Mary froze in the doorway, her breath catching in her throat as her eyes fell on Harvey bent over the files, his hand stuffing coded slips into his jacket. The colour drained from her face, her wide eyes stark with terror. For an instant she looked like a child caught in the dark — lips parted, hands trembling at her sides — before Briggs shoved past her, his voice a bark, breaking the spell. Mary's expression lingered, etched with the shock of betrayal and the dreadful realisation that the whispers of a traitor had been true all along.

Commander Briggs stormed in, armed sailors at his heels. Harvey stiffened, eyes darting for escape, but the rifles were already raised.

"Lieutenant Harvey," Briggs barked, voice like steel. "You are under arrest for treason."

For the first time, Harvey faltered. His jaw tightened, his shoulders sagged. As the sailors seized him, Nancy exhaled a breath she hadn't realised she was holding. Briggs turned to her. His moustache twitched, as if he disliked what he was about to say. "Miss Carter, it seems we owe you an apology."

Nancy didn't answer. She watched as Harvey was dragged out, the logbook clutched tightly in Briggs's hand. Around her, the wireless hissed and popped as if nothing had happened.

Briggs found Nancy outside the hut, the night air sharp against the faint glow of dawn. He looked awkward, his cap in his hands, his broad shoulders hunched as though the weight of his earlier doubt still pressed on him. "Carter," he began, his voice gruff, "I owe you more than a word. You saw what the rest of us couldn't. I dismissed you, and that near cost us all." He cleared his throat, eyes flicking away before meeting hers again. "You were right. You've been right all along. For what it's worth, I'll not make the mistake of underestimating you again." There was no flourish in his words, no polish — just the rough, plain honesty of a man humbled by the truth.

Just as Briggs finished speaking, the crunch of polished boots on gravel broke the silence. Commander Talbot stepped out from the shadows of the hut, hands clasped neatly behind his back, his cap set at a precise angle. He regarded Nancy with that same sharp, appraising look that had so often made her feel small, his moustache twitching as though he were weighing his words. For a long moment he said nothing, only studied her as though she were another report laid open on his desk.

At last he inclined his head, the gesture clipped, almost reluctant. "You've done what I said I would do," he admitted, his voice even but edged with formality. "I told you we'd smoke them out, yet it seems you've managed it yourself. Not many would have stood their ground as you did, Carter." He drew a measured breath, his pale eyes narrowing. "It appears I underestimated you too. I won't again."

He straightened his cuffs, the movement precise, and with a curt nod turned back toward the hut, leaving the faint scent of tobacco in his wake.

Mary touched her arm gently. "You were right." The startled, scared look on her face, now more relaxed, with a hint of dis-belief as to what she had just witnessed.

Nancy sighed, she didn't feel triumph. Only exhaustion. A sick, hollow relief that it was finally over.

Out at sea, Fred was still fighting his battles. Here, Nancy had fought hers. Both wars, she realised, left scars no one could see.

⚓

The news travelled through the base faster than any signal. By the time Nancy walked into the mess that evening, every head seemed to lift at once. Conversations faltered, then resumed in hushed tones as eyes followed her across the room. She felt the weight of it—curiosity, relief, and a prickling embarrassment from those who had once doubted her.

Florence, usually quick with a joke at Nancy's expense, shuffled over with a cigarette in hand. "Nancy… I—I owe you an apology. You were right about Harvey. I didn't want to believe it."

Another girl chimed in, nodding furiously. "None of us did. We thought you were chasing shadows."

Nancy smiled faintly, though it didn't quite reach her eyes. "I only did what any of us would have done, if we'd seen the signs."

She knew it wasn't true—not everyone would have pressed on through the whispers, the sidelong glances, the quiet ridicule. Not everyone could have. Now, with Harvey under guard and the whole ugly business laid bare, the same voices that had doubted her suddenly sought her approval.

Even Iris, as she made her way over to Nancy, to put forward an apology.

"Nancy, I'm sorry. Honestly, I thought it was all in your head, that or…" Iris stopped herself and shook her head. "I am sorry, and I admire your bravery. I briefly thought that perhaps I was under your suspicions, the way you held glances at me. I know we have never really seen eye to eye, but I admire what you did. The risk. It took courage." Iris held out her hand to shake Nancy's, in a manner of putting the past to bed.

As she sat down, plates shifted to make room, shoulders leaned closer in guilty camaraderie. The mess, once a place where she had felt the sting of isolation, now buzzed with tentative warmth. Nancy let it wash over her, but inside she remained steady, reserved. Nancy held the thought: respect given in hindsight carried less weight than conviction held in the moment. Still, she accepted their apologies with grace, knowing that tonight, at least, she had earned more than a place at the table.

The barracks were quiet when Nancy finally slipped back to her bunk. The laughter and chatter from the mess had faded to a low hum somewhere down the hall, leaving only the soft creak of floorboards and the bluster of the wind outside. She sat on the edge of her bed, tugging off her shoes, and let the calm settle around her.

They had meant their apologies—she knew that. The looks on their faces, the awkward sincerity in their voices, all spoke of genuine remorse. Yet the satisfaction she ought to have felt sat uneasily in her chest. Vindication was supposed to taste sweet. Instead, it carried a dull bitterness.

She thought of the long evenings when she had sat alone, dismissed and doubted, her suspicions waved away as nerves. The memory of that isolation clung like smoke on the horizon, a shadow that refused to lift. No chorus of apologies could erase how sharp that loneliness had felt.

Nancy drew the blanket tight around her shoulders and closed her eyes. Harvey was unmasked, the danger past, and she had been proven right… but victory felt quieter than she had imagined—lonelier, too. Tomorrow the world would go on, the war would grind forward, and she would return to her desk and her headphones. Still, tonight, she allowed herself a single satisfied breath of pride. Against odds, whispers, and doubt, she had held her ground. That, perhaps, was enough.

Nancy held one final thought before catching sleep. With all the doubt of her well-intended behaviours, all the suspicions and gossip… Would Fred have believed her?

⚓

The mess deck smelled of tea leaves and tobacco, the air thick with pipe smoke. Fred sat hunched over the table, letters spread before him. The mail had caught up with them at last, battered envelopes smudged from too many hands.

He had saved Nancy's for last.

Her handwriting steadied him before he even broke the seal. He could picture her bent over the page, hair escaping its pins, brow furrowed in concentration. For a moment, he almost forgot the roll of the sea beneath his boots.

He unfolded the letter and began to read.

My Dearest Fred,

I hardly know how to put this into words. Do you remember when you asked if I trusted the people around me? I wanted to, with all my heart. Turns out I was right to doubt. The man who questioned me, who all but called me a liar — he was the one. Harvey. He was feeding them wrong figures, sending our ships to slaughter. They caught him at last. Now they tell me I was right all along.

It should feel like a victory, but it doesn't. Too many lives have already been lost, and I keep thinking of the nights I sat at the wireless, hearing cries in the static. How many losses were his doing? How many men never came home because we trusted the wrong person?

They apologised to me, if that means anything. I thought of you when they said it. How you always believed in me, even when others did not. That's what kept me steady. You. Always you. Stay safe, I can't wait utill you are back home.

Yours,

Nancy

Fred lowered the letter slowly, his chest tight. Around him, the mess buzzed with low laughter and clinking mugs, but the words on the page drowned them out.

Harvey. A man in a uniform like his own, betraying them from within. It explained too much — convoys that vanished, signals that never made sense, battles they seemed doomed to lose before they'd begun.

Fred thought of the faces of men lost in the black water. He clenched his jaw, fighting down the rage, the bitterness that rose in him. *It wasn't only the U-boats that killed them. It was him… Harvey.*

He ran a hand over his eyes, then looked back at Nancy's words. A warmth pushed through the cold knot in his gut. Whatever hell the sea threw at him, whatever shadows Nancy faced ashore, they were bound by something Harvey could never touch.

Fred folded the letter carefully, tucking it inside his jacket where he kept the things that mattered most.

He whispered under his breath, unheard in the noise of the mess:

"I'll come back to you, Nance. I swear it."

Fred closed his eyes and drew in a long, weary breath, the salt tang of the sea mixed with the scent of tobacco filling his lungs. For a heartbeat he let the weight press on him — the loss, the fear, the gnawing guilt that never left him, and the shock of the latest news. Then he exhaled slowly, forcing it all down into the quiet place where he buried such things. With a sigh, he straightened, squaring his shoulders. The ship still needed him, the men still looked to him, and there was no room for weakness or frustration here. He set his cap firm on his head and turned to head back to the deck, resuming his duties as though the moment of weariness had never been.

JUNO

The convoy scattered westward, the battered freighters peeling off one by one toward their ports, their decks scarred but afloat. For days, HMS *Fury* had circled them like a sheepdog — herding, guarding, fighting off the wolves in the fog. Now, with the convoy delivered, she steamed back into Scapa Flow, her hull streaked with rust, her guns fouled with salt.

The men expected a brief respite — hot food, hammocks, perhaps even a night ashore — word filtered through the mess decks faster than any signal: leave was cancelled. There would be no rest this time.

Fred heard it confirmed on the bridge. "New orders," the captain said flatly. "We're to join Force G. Channel operations. Support landings." His tone was brisk, but his eyes betrayed the weight of it. Fred knew this was coming, he knew the training exercise before the most recent convoy was building for this. This moment. This operation.

When the order came down, the words hit Fred harder than the North Atlantic gales ever had. Juno. The name alone was enough to make his stomach turn cold. It was no longer rumour or guesswork—it was written into their course, their duty, their fate. A hollow weight settled in his chest as the realisation struck: every drill, every convoy, every sleepless night had been leading to this. He thought of the men around him—faces he knew as well as his own by now—and wondered how many of them would see home again. For a moment, the ship's familiar thrum felt different beneath his boots, not the steady heartbeat of survival, but the drumbeat of something vast and unstoppable, carrying them toward fire and chaos.

The Channel. The invasion everyone had whispered of, the "big show" spoken about with forced bravado. Now it was real.

Fred found Jack leaning against the bulkhead, a cigarette burning low between his fingers. The look on his face told Fred he didn't need to break the news.

"So it's true then," Jack said quietly, eyes fixed on the deck plates. "Juno."

Fred nodded, his throat tight. "Straight away."

For a moment neither man spoke, the silence heavier than words. Then Jack exhaled, a thin stream of smoke curling upward. "Bloody hell. Always knew it was coming. Just didn't think it'd be us."

Fred swallowed, his voice low. "Feels different, doesn't it? Like we've been walking toward it all along, and now the road's run out. Suddenly."

Jack flicked his cigarette into the scupper, grinding it under his heel. "Aye. Well… all we can do now is hold tight." His tone was firm, but Fred caught the flicker in his eyes—the same dread that gripped him, the same realisation neither of them could shake.

On the deck, the boys tried to cover their nerves with laughter. “About time we give Jerry a bloody nose!” one said, slapping his mate on the back. Others smoked in silence, staring at the deck plates. They knew what awaited: air attacks, mines, coastal guns, and the black maw of the Channel itself.

Fred stood at the stern, near the depth charge rack, that evening, watching the sun sink over the Flow. He thought of Nancy, of their one day together under a gentler sun. He hadn’t told her where he was bound — he hadn’t needed to. She would know, the way she always seemed to.

The sea shifted beneath him, the destroyer answering her engines as she turned toward the south. The time of waiting was over. HMS *Fury* was bound for France.

The destroyer rode at anchor with the rest of the fleet, dark shapes crowding the Channel as far as Fred could see. Warships, landing craft, troopships heavy with men — an armada gathered in silence, waiting for dawn.

Below decks, there was no silence. The mess deck hummed with nervous energy. Cards slapped against the table, mugs clattered, voices rose in forced cheer. Some men laughed too loud, their jokes brittle. Others sat hunched over letters, pencils scratching as if the act of writing might ward off what tomorrow would bring.

Fred moved among them, ducking the low beams, exchanging a word here, a hand on the shoulder there. He paused by Harris — the freckled lad who had panicked during the last convoy attack. The boy's hands trembled as he packed and repacked his kit bag, his face pale under the harsh lamplight.

"Easy, lad," Fred said, crouching beside him. "We're not boarding hell itself, just France."

Harris gave a nervous laugh, not quite convincing. "Feels much the same, sir."

Fred clapped him gently on the back. "We've trained for this. You'll do as you've always done — your part, no more, no less. That's all any of us can."

Around them, the wardroom clock ticked too loud. Someone began a song — off-key but defiant — and others joined in, their voices rising to cover the fear. Fred couldn't hide the smile growing on his face, and he thought of his friend Harry, wondering if he too would be headed to the beaches of France, singing out of tune.

When Fred returned topside, the deck was cold, the sea restless under a moon shrouded in cloud. He leaned over an old oil drum, staring out across the black water toward the coast he couldn't yet see. He thought of Nancy — her laugh in the spring sunshine, the weight of her hand in his — and he let the memory settle over him like armour.

Below, his men were afraid. So was he. Come dawn, fear would not matter. *Fury* had her orders, and they would carry them through.

For almost fourteen days the world was nothing but smoke, thunder, and salt. *Fury* prowled the grey waters off Juno Beach, her guns barking until the barrels glowed, her decks slick with spent casings. The air stank of cordite and burning oil, of seaweed churned up by shells and the sour tang of fear.

The noise never stopped. The crash of naval guns, the whine of shells overhead, the drone of aircraft diving low. Men shouted orders until their voices broke, the clang of steel and the rattle of chains punctuating every hour. Sleep came in snatches, hammocks swaying above mess tables still littered with mugs of cold tea.

The sea itself turned hostile. Wreckage drifted on the tide — broken rafts, lifebelts, the bodies of men carried out from the beaches. Fred forced himself not to look too long when they passed, but the crew saw them too, their laughter fading until even their jokes turned hollow.

On the beaches, France burned. Flames leapt from devastated villages; smoke rolled inland like storm clouds. The tide brought in more landing craft, more men, more casualties. *Fury* ferried messages, screened the transports, fired until her magazines ran low, then fired again once resupplied.

By the end of the week the ship was scarred — paint blistered from heat, hull scraped from near misses with mines, her crew hollow-eyed with exhaustion. Yet still she fought, because there was no other choice.

At night, when the guns at last fell silent for an hour, the dark waves heaving beneath him. He could still hear it — the roar, the cries, the endless thrashing. He knew that Nancy, miles away in

Scotland, would never truly imagine what this coast had cost.

The morning broke deceptively calm. The Channel rolled beneath a low sky, smoke drifting in lazy bands from the burning coast. *Fury* steamed south of Juno Beach, her decks blackened from almost two week's bombardment, her men moving like shadows — weary, salt-stained, but steady.

Fred stood on the bridge, the binoculars heavy in his hands. Ahead, the sea looked clear, only broken by the wakes of landing craft scurrying to and from the beachhead. Yet every man aboard knew the danger hadn't passed. Mines. Invisible, patient, waiting just below the surface.

They had been told the area was "swept and clear." Fred knew better. Mines lurked like ghosts, invisible until it was too late.

"Steady as she goes," he called, eyes narrowing at the faint white wakes of landing craft ahead. His crew were bone-tired but alert — days of endless escort duty had taught them never to relax.

The lookout's voice cracked across the wind: *"Float ahead! Bearing green twenty!"*

Fred's heart lurched. He swung his glass. At first, he saw nothing but ripples. Then — the faint, bulbous shadow of a mine bobbing just beneath the swell, tethered to the seabed, its horned crown glinting wet in the sun.

"Hard a 'starboard!" the captain barked. The helmsman spun the wheel, the destroyer groaning as she turned. For a heartbeat it seemed they had cleared it — the shape sliding past the bow.

Then came the sound.

The first jolt came like a giant's fist.

"Mine!" someone screamed.

A blinding flash erupted to starboard, followed by a deafening roar that tore through steel and bone alike. Fred was thrown hard against the bulkhead, the taste of blood in his mouth. The destroyer heeled violently, alarms shrieking, smoke and flame bursting upward in a black column.

A sickening, metallic crack, followed by a roar that swallowed the world. The mine's blast erupted against *Fury*'s starboard side, tearing steel as though it were paper. The deck heaved under Fred's boots, a column of water and fire shooting skyward, cascading down in sheets.

Men were flung like ragdolls; screams lost in the thunder. The bridge windows shattered inward, glass cutting Fred's cheek. He clung to the rungs of the companionway ladder as the ship lurched, listing sharply, alarms shrieking through the hull.

"Damage control to starboard! Flooding forward compartments!"

The mess deck was already chaos. Water surged through the torn steel plate, black and stinking of oil. Men waded waist-deep, dragging the wounded, hauling lines, trying desperately to stem the torrent. A stoker's body floated against the bulkhead, his eyes wide, unseeing.

The deck pitched beneath his feet, slick with oil and seawater. Men staggered, some thrown over the side by the blast. Fred dragged himself upright, forcing his voice steady even as his ears rang.

"Damage control parties forward! Seal the bulkheads! Get those pumps running!" He repeated, as he stumbled toward the blown section of the ship. The bow was a mangled ruin — twisted plates, gaping holes where men had been moments before. The sea poured in, unstoppable. He saw one of his ratings pinned beneath debris, water rising fast around him. Without thinking, Fred threw himself down, bracing against the weight of the wreckage.

Above, the guns lay silent for the first time in days, their crews scrambling instead with axes and pumps. The stern dipped lower, the deck tilting, ropes and crates sliding toward the sea.

Fred fought his way down the ladder, the acrid stench of smoke and cordite clawing his lungs. "Steady, lads! Keep her balanced! We're not beaten yet!" His voice cut through the din, but even he knew the truth — the wound was mortal.

The captain's order came, tight and final. *"Abandon ship."*

The words struck harder than the blast.

The destroyer shuddered, listing harder. Fred knew the truth — they wouldn't save her. She was mortally wounded, like a beast struck through the heart. They, however, could still save men.

"Abandon forward sections!" he roared, voice raw. "Get them clear — move, damn you!"

Boats were swung out, scrambling men spilling into them, others clinging to rafts or plunging straight into the cold Channel. Fred stayed until the last, helping Harris and two others shove a lifeboat free, helping the boy toward safety.

The acrid smoke blurred his vision, and through it he thought of Nancy — the quiet way she had laughed at their first dance, the courage in her eyes when she'd written of standing her ground under fire. If this was the end, he prayed she'd never think he'd given less than everything.

Another explosion tore through the wreck, the deck pitching violently. Fred lost his footing, hitting the riveted seam of the bulkhead, hard. Strong hands seized his arm — one of his surviving officers dragging him back.

"Sir, we have to go!"

Only when the deck tilted sickeningly beneath him, water rushing up through the hatches, did Fred leap into the sea. Salt and oil filled his mouth, the roar of the wounded ship drowning out every other sound.

Behind them, the destroyer groaned like a dying animal, her bow sinking fast. The sea claimed her, flames hissing out as the water closed over.

From the water he looked back once. HMS *Fury* — battered, proud, faithful — listed hard, her hull torn wide, her funnels belching smoke. She groaned like a wounded beast, then slowly, inexorably, began to settle, her bow lifting as her stern was swallowed by the sea.

Fred clung to the side of a raft, gasping, heart breaking. He had known the line between safety and slaughter was thin — but watching *Fury* die, carrying men he could not save, he felt the truth in his bones.

The destroyer was gone.

Fred drifted in and out of consciousness, the world reduced to salt water burning in his lungs and the crushing ache in his chest. He was dimly aware of strong hands hauling him aboard a pitching corvette, men shouting, boots thudding on steel.

"Got him — he's breathing, just!"

Fred coughed hard, water and bile spilling from his mouth. Visions swam. Faces blurred above him, gas masks, helmets, hands pressing a bandage against his temple where blood slicked his hair.

His ship was gone. *Fury*. He knew it even before forcing his eyes to the horizon and saw only smoke and a patch of oil-streaked sea where she had been. The destroyer that had carried him through so much — that had been home and battle and brotherhood — was sinking into silence.

And men. God, so many men. The screams still rang in his ears. The weight of those he couldn't save pressed heavier than the sea.

"Lie still, sir," someone murmured. "You're safe now."

Fred knew better. He was alive, yes — and that was the cruelest part.

⚓

The wireless crackled with broken reports, voices urgent and half-swallowed by static. Nancy leaned closer, knuckles white against the desk.

"...destroyer mined... heavy casualties... survivors being taken off..."

Her pencil shook against the page, the words barely legible. Her throat closed. She wanted to scream, to demand the ship's name, but she could only sit frozen, hands trembling, ears straining for scraps.

The operator repeated it. Clearer this time. The name of Fred's ship.

Nancy's breath hitched. For a moment, the room seemed to tilt around her, the floor falling away.

Mary's hand touched her arm. "Nance? What is it? What did they say?"

Nancy pressed her lips together, unable to speak. The words on the page stared back at her like a death sentence.

Heavy casualties. Survivors being taken off.

Her heart ached to know if Fred was among them — but no signal came to tell her. Nothing but static, hissing, merciless, leaving her in the dark.

She folded the log slip slowly, too carefully, as though by neatness alone she could hold her world together. Then she whispered, so softly Mary almost didn't hear:

"Please, God. Not again."

Nancy's blood pulsed cold through her veins, as if the very heart had frozen in her chest. Her fingers stiffened around the pencil, her breath caught tight in her throat. For a moment the world seemed distant — the hum of the wireless, the murmur of voices in the hut — all drowned beneath the icy rush that gripped her. She forced herself to swallow, to stabilise her hand, but the chill lingered, reminding her with cruel clarity how close the war pressed in around her. All she thought, was of *Fred.*

THE THREAD THAT FRAYED

The dream came with such force it felt real. Nancy heard the door slam against the wind, boots striking the floorboards, and then Fred's voice—clear, steady, alive. She turned, heart pounding, and there he was in the dim light, rain glistening on his cap, blue eyes fixed on her as though he had never been away.

He crossed the room in two strides, swept her into his arms, and the world seemed to right itself. The scent of salt and oil clung to him, his uniform cold against her cheek, and she held tighter, desperate, as if by holding on she could keep the sea from ever taking him again. "You're safe," she gasped, the words breaking. "You're safe, Fred." He only smiled, murmuring that the danger was past, that nothing could tear them apart now.

His face blurred, his voice thinned into static, and his embrace dissolved like mist. The room darkened. She reached out, clawing at shadows, calling his name, but he was already gone.

Nancy jerked awake, breath caught in her throat, the taste of fear sharp on her tongue. The barracks ceiling stretched above, blank and unyielding, the silence broken only by the quiet breathing of the other Wrens. Her arms were empty, her skin clammy with cold sweat.

For a moment she could still feel the phantom weight of him, the warmth that wasn't there. A shudder ran through her as the truth pressed down: Fred was still out there, in the black water, in reach of death with every passing hour. The dream had been a cruel trick; a glimpse of safety she dared not hope for.

Nancy buried her face in the pillow, fists clenched tight, fighting the terror that rose like a tide. The fear was always there, waiting for her in the dark—but never so sharp as when she had tasted what it was to believe him safe.

The dormitory was quieter these days. Too quiet.

Nancy moved through it in silence, the empty bunks speaking louder than any voice could. Names crossed off the board, belongings packed away by trembling hands. Letters that would never be delivered now tucked in drawers, gathering dust. She had learned not to linger, not to count the spaces where laughter used to live.

Her own letters — letters to Fred — lay untouched in her locker, the last one over a week old. The envelope was creased from her fingers. Sat, waiting, since the report. Destroyer mined. Heavy casualties. Survivors taken off. No names. No certainty.

In the nights after Juno, when no news came and her thoughts threatened to swallow her whole, Nancy found herself turning again and again to Fred's letters. She kept them bundled neatly with a ribbon, tucked beneath her pillow, as though having them close might anchor him to her. When the darkness pressed too heavy, she would slip one free, unfolding the creased paper carefully, smoothing it across her lap as if it were something fragile.

She read the words slowly, lips moving silently over his handwriting, though she already knew every line by heart. Each sentence carried his voice back to her—the little turns of phrase, the dry humour, the way he always ended with *Yours always*. Sometimes the words calmed her enough to steady her breathing; sometimes they blurred as her eyes stung with tears. When sleep refused to come, she would begin again, reading and re-reading until exhaustion finally dragged her under. It became her ritual, her way of keeping him near, of holding back the terror of not knowing whether he was lost to her or still out there on the sea, fighting to return.

Every night she walked past the wireless hut, the hiss of static leaking through the door. Sometimes she sat at her post until dawn, headphones pressed so tight they bruised her ears, straining for a voice that never came. Her pencil hovered over the pad, waiting to write his name, his call sign — anything to prove he still existed in the black water — but the airwaves gave her nothing.

Mary tried to offer comfort, in her way. A hand on Nancy's shoulder, a cup of weak tea pressed into her palm. "You have to rest, Nance. You'll make yourself ill."

Nancy only shook her head. Rest meant remembering. Work meant forgetting.

So she worked. Logging every fragment of German code, every broken transmission, her handwriting sharp and relentless. If she couldn't save Fred, she would save someone else. She would not let another ship go blind because she faltered.

One night, alone in the hut, she pulled the headphones off and stared at her reflection in the dark window. Hollow eyes, skin pale in the lamplight, lips pressed tight. A woman she barely recognised.

Edward's ghost lingered in that glass, the boyish grin she'd lost too soon. For months she had lived with his absence like a second shadow. Now Fred's absence pressed beside it, heavy and unbearable.

She closed her eyes, slowing her breath. No. Not again. The war would not take him from her, this opportunity, her second chance of happiness.

Whether he lived or not, Fred had given her something Edward's death had stolen — hope. Fragile, reckless hope. She clung to it now with both hands, even if it cut her palms raw.

Lifting her chin, she whispered into the static-filled room:

"You're not gone, Fred. Not until I see it with my own eyes. I won't stop fighting for you."

The words vanished into the night, unheard by anyone but her. Yet for the first time in weeks, she felt the faintest flicker of strength return.

She would keep listening. She would keep working. She would not let the war hollow her out completely.

⚓

The church smelled faintly of stone dust and candle wax, the air cold despite the on-set of summer and the press of bodies in the pews. Sunlight filtered through the stained glass in muted shards of red and gold, falling across bowed heads and folded hands.

The vicar's voice carried steadily down the nave, words of comfort, of endurance, of God's will—but for Nancy they were hollow syllables, passing over her without meaning.

Beside her, Mary mouthed the hymns, her voice a soft thread lost in the swell of the congregation. Nancy held the hymnbook open but didn't sing. Her lips stayed still, her eyes fixed on the pages as though the notes might rearrange into answers if she stared long enough.

Once, she had believed—believed in the justice of God, in the certainty of prayer, in the promise that good would prevail. War however, had gnawed at that faith, stripped it bare. Too many telegrams. Too many empty chairs at the mess table. Too many nights when she whispered Fred's name into the dark and heard nothing in return.

Why? The question repeated itself in her head with every rise of the vicar's voice. Why should an almighty hand allow such waste, such cruelty, such endless grief? Why had she been given love only to have it dangled before her like a candle in the wind, threatening to go out at any moment?

The hymn ended, voices fell away, and the hush of prayer settled over the church. Nancy lowered her head, but no words came. Her silence was louder than any prayer she could muster.

Nancy closed her eyes, but no prayer rose to meet the silence. Instead there was only the echo of the vicar's words, drifting past her like smoke, impossible to catch hold of. She envied Mary's quiet devotion, the way her friend's lips moved with conviction, as if every line of scripture was stitched firmly into her heart.

For Nancy, that thread had frayed. She could not reconcile a God who allowed torpedoes to rip ships apart, who let mothers bury sons, who let women wait in silence for men who never came home. Her faith had once been her anchor, but now it felt like another cruel trick—something that promised safety yet slipped away the moment she reached for it.

Yet, beneath the bitterness, something in her still resisted letting go completely. Perhaps it was habit, perhaps desperation. A part of her still wanted to believe there was meaning, that Fred's life—and hers—were not just at the mercy of blind chance and steel.

When the final hymn began, Nancy rose with the others. Her voice did not join theirs, but she stood, rigid, a lone figure in the swell of sound. For now, faith eluded her, but in the quiet chamber of her heart, she left the door ajar, if only barely—because if Fred came home, if love could survive the war, then perhaps so too could belief.

The path crunched the same under their boots, but the world felt altered. The gulls still wheeled overhead, the harbour still glimmered with grey steel, but to Nancy everything looked drained of colour, as if the war had finally bled the brightness out of the day.

Mary kept her arm looped through Nancy's, holding her close. She didn't chatter the way she usually did. The silence between them was heavy, filled with things neither of them wanted to say aloud.

Nancy's eyes drifted to the anchorage. Destroyers shifted at their moorings, crews shouting faintly across the water. She found herself searching the horizon, half-expecting to see Fred's ship appear out of the mist. Nevertheless the sea remained empty.

Her throat ached. "They said survivors," she whispered, more to herself than to Mary. "They said some were taken off."

Mary squeezed her arm tighter. "Then hold on to that, Nance. Don't let go of it."

Nancy swallowed hard. Edward had once been missing too — until the telegram came. She could still see the black-edged paper, the careful words that had ended everything. Missing in action, presumed killed. She had told herself she would never endure that again.

Now here she was, waiting once more, her heart twisting in the same cruel vice.

They paused at the edge of the path, the sea breeze stinging their faces. Nancy's hands trembled as she pulled her greatcoat tighter. "I can't do this again, Mary. Not with him. If he's gone—" Her voice cracked, and she turned her face away, ashamed of the tears burning her eyes.

Mary pulled her close, wrapping both arms around her, holding on fiercely. "You can," she said, her own voice shaking. "Because you did it before, and you're still here… and because… because I think he's coming back to you. I just do."

Nancy let the sob escape then, muffled against her friend's shoulder. The gulls cried overhead, the sea lapped at the harbour wall, and somewhere far out beyond the horizon men lived or died in silence.

Nance… you can't carry the whole war on your shoulders, love. None of us can. All we can do is keep faith that the sea gives them back to us." Mary said softly after a silence between them.

"But what if it doesn't? What if he's already—" Her voice trembling.

"Don't. Don't finish that. You'll tie yourself in knots with what-ifs. He's too stubborn to be taken, you know that. I've seen the way he looks at you — no U-boat in the Atlantic could stand a chance against that." Mary cut in, gently, before Nancy could finish pouring the words from her mouth.

Nancy let out a shaky laugh despite herself, wiping her eyes.

"You always make it sound so simple." She said, as she steadied herself.

"It is simple. Until you've got proof to the contrary, you hold onto hope. That's the only ration we get that never runs out." Mary smiled softly, squeezing Nancy's arm.

She closed her eyes, clinging to Mary's words like driftwood. Fragile hope — but hope all the same.

Weeks slipped by in a haze, each one bleeding into the next until Nancy could scarcely tell Sunday from Thursday. The rhythm of duty—headphones pressed to her ears, pencils scratching, messages carried up and down the corridor—kept her body moving, but her mind wandered endlessly to the same place. Every time a door creaked open, every time footsteps echoed down the hall, she found herself holding her breath, daring to hope that Fred might be the one to appear. She pictured him filling the doorway, his smile breaking through the grey monotony, his presence enough to set the world alight again. It was that fragile hope, however foolish, that kept her steady when the silence of his absence threatened to crush her.

THROUGH EVERY STORM

Each morning began the same: Nancy's boots carrying her down to the harbour, to sit beneath the clocktower, before her shift, breathing in the fresh morning air, eyes straining for any sign of him. The quayside was always alive with movement — trawlers unloading their catch, merchantmen limping in with salt-streaked hulls, mailbags slung ashore by weary hands — but never the ship she longed to see. She lingered anyway, scanning faces, searching the letters pinned up at the post office window, clutching at scraps of gossip from sailors on leave. Then, with hope bruised but not broken, she turned back toward the signals hut, headphones and static waiting, her heart ticking to the same endless question: *Would today be the day Fred came home?*

Time had taken on a strange, elastic quality. Hours at her post in the signals hut stretched unbearably long, while the moments at the harbour seemed to vanish in an instant. Nancy's heart leapt each time she saw a destroyer round the headland, only to sink again when she realised it wasn't his. She scolded herself for such foolishness—ships did not return on the strength of one girl's longing—but she couldn't help it. Hope had become her lifeline, fragile though it was, a thread she clung to against the pull of despair.

Each evening ended the same: her eyes fixed on the horizon long after her shift was done, as though the sea itself might yield an answer if only she stared hard enough.

Sometimes Mary came with her, chattering to keep the silence at bay, linking arms with a warmth that steadied Nancy against the chill feeling. Mary would chatter about the small things—what was served in the mess, which officer had lost his temper, the latest letter from home—anything to lighten the heaviness of waiting. Yet even her brightness faltered at times, her gaze drifting to the same horizon, her smile dimming. On rainy mornings, Mary stayed behind, but Nancy came regardless, coat soaked through, hair plastered to her face, refusing to let weather or reason deny her the chance that Fred might return. Each evening Nancy would be found standing stubbornly beneath the clocktower overlooking the harbour, knowing that's where Fred would know to find her, until the cold of evening settled deep in her bones. No letter, no signal, no figure striding up the quay ever came, yet still she waited. Hope, however fragile, was harder to put down than the heaviest burden.

Around the base, the mood was much the same. Every letter that arrived was opened with trembling hands; every knock at the door set hearts racing with dread. Sailors came and went, some swaggering with relief, others walking heavily, eyes shadowed by what they had seen. The constant rumble of the war filled every corner—distant explosions at sea, the drone of planes overhead, the clipped voices of officers passing orders. For Nancy, all of it blurred into a single ache of anticipation: the endless, desperate wait for one man's return.

⚓

Nancy had almost stopped believing in reunions. There had been too many nights spent listening to the wireless crackle with reports of ships lost, convoys scattered, names read in trembling voices. She had learned not to hope too loudly.

That morning, as she did every morning, these last few weeks, she hurried across the harbour yard with the gulls crying overhead, she caught sight of the small fleet easing back into port — all battered, paint scarred with salt and fire, but afloat.

Her heart lurched.

Nancy had heard murmurs, rumours of a fleet returning, carrying the survivors from the invasion, almost a month ago now. She had obtained leave to see the men home. To see if…

The gangways clattered into place, none of the ships were *Fury*. Men began to file down. Exhausted faces, some grinning through grime, others hollow-eyed. Nancy searched every one, her pulse quickening painfully.

Nancy's eyes swept the harbour as they always did, but this time something stilled her breath. A familiar stride, a familiar tilt of the shoulders against the wind—Fred. For a heartbeat she didn't believe it, afraid her longing had conjured a mirage from the spray and the bustle of men disembarking. Then he turned, his face catching the light, and certainty struck her with such force she gripped the handrail to steady herself. Relief and disbelief tangled inside her until she felt almost faint.

Fred looked older somehow, thinner in the face, eyes shadowed. His cap not upon his head or tucked under his arm, and his uniform was tatty, not crisp how she would usually expect to see him — but it was him — unmistakably him.

Nancy didn't think. She ran. The yard blurred around her as she pushed through the crowd. She didn't remember crossing the cobbles, only the pounding of her boots and the relentless drum of her heartbeat. The harbour seemed to narrow around them, every sound—shouted orders, gulls crying, the crash of the tide—fading into nothing. Her hair flew loose behind her as she ran, and when she reached him she stopped short, breath caught in her throat, afraid that if she touched him he might vanish like all the dreams she'd woken from. He saw her in the crowd, halfway down, and for a moment he froze, as though afraid she were a mirage. Then he broke into a tired, crooked smile — the same smile that had haunted her through every sleepless night.

They met in the yard, stopping short. For an instant, neither spoke. The chaos seemed to hush around them, the gulls, the sea, the shouting sailors fading into nothing.

The sight of her was like breaking the surface after too long underwater. He had pictured this moment through endless black nights at sea, but no imagining came close to the truth of Nancy standing there, eyes shining with tears and fury and joy all at once. Relief swelled in his chest so sharply it almost hurt, and for a heartbeat he could do nothing but absorb the vision of her — the familiar set of her shoulders, the way her hands trembled as if she couldn't quite believe he was real. He wanted to speak, to apologise for every moment she had spent in dread, but all the words tangled uselessly; only the sheer miracle of being here, with her, remained.

Fred reached for her first, hands strong and sure as they pulled her into his chest. She melted into him, her cheek pressed against the rough wool of his coat, the scent of salt and smoke clinging to him like proof of where he had been. His arms wrapped around her with a fierce certainty, as though he too feared the world might snatch them apart again. Nancy let out a sob that was half-laughter, half-grief, her body trembling with the sheer weight of exasperated relief.

For a moment neither of them spoke. Words seemed clumsy, unnecessary. Everything they had endured—the waiting, the silence, the unspoken fears—hung in that embrace. When Fred finally pulled back, just enough to look at her, his eyes were glassy with exhaustion but alive with something brighter.

Nancy's throat ached with everything unsaid. She wanted to tell him more about Harvey, about the accusations, about the nights she thought she'd never see him again. She wanted to tell him she loved him. All she could manage in that moment was a whisper:

"You came back."

Fred reached for her hand, rough and calloused, gripping hers with a desperation that said more than words ever could. His eyes glistened, the survivor's guilt weighing heavy, but in them was also something fierce — relief, hunger, hope.

"I promised, didn't I?" he said, voice hoarse.

Nancy felt her knees weaken. Her eyes swell, the hot tears running down her puffed cheeks. Fred took her chin in his hand and wiped his thumb across her cheeks to steal away all her tears.

All around, the harbour moved on—sailors calling greetings, officers directing the unloading, the roar of machinery of war, smoke drifting across the water. Still, for Nancy and Fred, time had slowed. The war had not ended; danger still loomed. Yet in that single moment, with the gulls circling overhead and the sea rolling endlessly beyond, love had carved out its own fragile sanctuary.

Nancy realised, with a clarity that steadied her, that even in the midst of chaos, love had found a way through.

Exasperated relief rushed through her, so fierce it nearly took her knees from under her. For weeks she had braced herself for the telegram, for the silence, for the cold certainty of loss — and instead here he was, flesh and breath and warmth before her. The tension she had carried like armour cracked all at once, leaving her laughing and crying in the same breath, unable to decide whether to scold him for making her wait or simply cling to him and never let go.

The harbour quieted as evening fell. The smoke had thinned, the shouts of men and clatter of stretchers fading into the distance. Fred stood by a bench near the seawall, his jacket draped loosely around his shoulders, his face pale with exhaustion but alive.

Nancy stood beside him, unable to stop touching him — her hand brushing his sleeve, his hair, as if proving again and again that he was real. For weeks she had imagined this moment and feared it in equal measure. Now that it was here, words seemed harder than ever.

Fred turned, his eyes searching hers. "You don't have to stay," he murmured, voice still hoarse from smoke and seawater. "You've already done more than enough."

She swallowed hard, her chest aching with all the things she'd left unsaid. For Edward. For fear. For pride. No more. The war had stolen too much already.

"Fred," she whispered, her hand tightening on his. "I need you to hear this."

His brows furrowed, but he said nothing.

"I love you." The words tumbled out, fierce and certain, cutting through the salt sting in her throat. "I've been so afraid… afraid to lose you, afraid to betray what I had before, but I can't lose this chance. Not again. I love you, and if the sea takes you tomorrow, at least you'll know it."

Fred's breath caught. Then, slowly, he lifted her hand to his lips, pressing it against his mouth with a reverence that nearly undid her. His eyes shone, raw and unguarded.

"I've been waiting to hear you say that," he said softly. "Through every storm, every night out there, that's what I held on to."

Nancy leaned into him, closing the last space between them.

Fred drew her into his arms, holding her as though he might never let go again. A tight embrace. The world around them seemed to fall away, leaving only the sound of her breath against his chest, the reassuring beat of his heart beneath his uniform. He lowered his head and pressed a gentle kiss to her forehead, lingering there as if sealing the moment in memory.

Around them, the harbour creaked and sighed, the smell of smoke still in the air, but in that moment, there was only this: two survivors, clinging to something stronger than the war that had tried to tear them apart.

Fred whispered, the words steady and certain, carrying the weight of every mile of sea and storm that had kept them apart.

"I love you, Nancy."

THE DOCK HOUSE

April – 1946

The old dock house sat snug against the Weaver riverbank, its brick walls softened by moss and ivy, the windows glistening faintly with drizzle. Beyond, the river slid by in an easy, unhurried current, its surface rippling with the patter of spring rain. The air carried the scent of damp earth and budding greenery, the kind of gentle freshness that promised new beginnings.

The house smelled faintly of coal smoke and fresh bread. Outside, spring rain pattered against the windowpanes, dripping from the hedgerows that lined the narrow lane. Nancy stood at the sink, drying the last of the breakfast dishes, and listened to the stable hum of peace.

Peace. After years of static and gunfire and sirens, the silence still startled her.

She glanced over her shoulder. Fred was in the garden, knelt among the flowerbeds, his jacket discarded on a chair, sleeves rolled past his elbows. Raindrops clung to his hair, catching the light as he tugged weeds free with steady determination., wrestling weeds with the same grim determination he had once turned on U-boats. The puppy bounded around him in delighted chaos, tail wagging furiously, snatching at the roots Fred tossed aside as if they were prizes. Every so often, Fred paused to laugh, his voice carrying warmly across the garden, softened by the drizzle.

Nancy smiled, warmth blooming in her chest.

Nancy set the freshly baked loaf on the sill to cool, the yeasty warmth filling the kitchen. She wiped her hands on her apron and lingered, admiring the way her wedding band gleamed against her flour-dusted fingers. It was still new enough that she caught herself twisting it gently, as though checking it was real, not some fragile dream conjured during the long, lonely war years. The kitchen clock ticked steadily, and for once, time felt generous.

The war had taken so much — Edward's laughter, friends whose names were etched on village memorials, a part of her own youth she could never reclaim. Yet it had given her this too: a second chance, hard-won, fragile, precious.

On the cabinet lay a small bundle of letters, tied with ribbon. Fred's handwriting, hers, their war distilled into ink and paper. Sometimes, when the nights were long and the wind howled, Nancy still read them. Not to remember the fear — but to remind herself of how fiercely they had clung to life, to love, when the world was burning.

She stepped to the door, opening it onto the garden. Pushing it with her left hand, she paused briefly in a moment of echo, again admiring the golden band on her left-hand ring finger. Nancy smiled to herself. As she pushed the door open, it gave a gentle creak. Fred straightened, wiping his brow with the back of his hand, and his eyes found hers. That same steady gaze, shadowed by everything he had seen, yet bright with something unbreakable.

Their eyes met, and Nancy felt the same warmth that had steadied her through the war, now deepened by the knowledge they had come through it—together. Fred smiled, simple and sure, and in that small, ordinary moment, Nancy realised she had everything she had once dared to hope for: love, home, and safety.

"Tea soon?" he asked, his voice carrying over the drizzle.

"Tea soon," she called back, her throat tight with a sudden, grateful ache.

Nancy crouched low, hand outstretched, and the tiny border collie tumbled across the flagstones toward her, paws too big for its legs. She laughed through the sting of tears as it stumbled into her arms, wriggling with uncontrolled joy. Standing in the doorway to the back garden, she felt a warmth she had thought the war had stolen forever.

The war was over. The scars would never fade entirely, but here, in the soft green of a new spring, they had made it home.

Home. Safe. Together.

THE END

Acknowledgements:

Firstly, I wish to thank my great-grandmother, Nancy Oakes, whom I was fortunate enough to know for over twenty-two years of my life - may she rest in peace, love, and eternal happiness with her husband, Fred Oakes.

I fondly remember her stories of the war, she would share with me, when I was younger, telling stories of people, events and experiences, I have tried to recall and include many of these within this book. I also must thank her for being the only person who would make me a cup of tea with four sugars, no questions — though I don't drink tea anymore.

Nancy has inspired numerous aspects of my life, and I would like to think that the woman she was, lives on within myself, not least, her stories inspired me to take avid interest in history, maritime warfare and the second world war.

I would like to thank my family, for their support, in particular, my mother (Alison Oakes) for helping proof-read. I appreciate you!

I should also note that OpenAI provided assistance with spelling, grammar, and some small editorial suggestions — an invaluable aid to a dyslexic like me.

Here I wish also to thank Rebeka (Beki) Birchall, for her creation of the artwork for this book – a talented artist and close friend, thank you!

Finally, I thank you, dear reader, for choosing to pick up this book, and for allowing the stories of real people and real events to live on, long after they might otherwise have been forgotten.

A.A.Woodward

This is a work of fiction. Inspired by true events during WW2; some creative liberties have been taken for storytelling purposes.

ISBN: 978-1-9193194-0-7

Published by A.A.Woodward
Edited with assistance from AI tools for grammar and proofing support

Printed in the United Kingdom
First edition, 2025

Printed and bound in the United Kingdom
16/10/2025
01977176-0002